The
Ayre
Conspiracy

by
Roy Porter

Grosvenor House
Publishing Limited

This book is published by
Grosvenor House Publishing Ltd
Link House
140 The Broadway, Tolworth, Surrey, KT6 7HT.
www.grosvenorhousepublishing.co.uk

This book is a work of fiction. Any resemblance to
people or events, past or present, is purely coincidental.

A CIP record for this book
is available from the British Library

ISBN 978-1-78623-195-6

The Isle of Man, known affectionately as 'the jewel in the Irish Sea', lies mid-way between Ireland and the North of England. It is approximately 32 miles long and about 15 miles wide. The capital is Douglas, and in 1994, the island had a population of around 75,000. The indigenous inhabitants were known as Manx, and their name for the island was Ellan Vannin, also known simply as Mann. It is a self-governing Crown dependency, although the head of state is Queen Elizabeth II, who holds the title of Lord of Mann. The Lord of Mann is represented by a Lieutenant Governor although foreign relations and defence are the responsibility of the British Government.

The Point of Ayre (Manx: Kione ny h-Ayrey) is the northernmost part of the island and is the closest point on the Isle of Man to the British mainland; Burrow Head in Scotland. The name Ayre comes from the Norse word *Eyrr* meaning gravel bank. Strong currents offshore cause an ever-changing build-up of shingle, so the beach changes shape with each tide.

Cover picture courtesy of Ray Collister
(Ray Collister Photography, Isle of Man)

Chapter 1 - The Old House

The official name of 'The Old House' was Kingsway Mansion, a name going back to Tudor times, when the Kingsway family built it near the Point of Ayre, the northernmost point of the Isle of Man. Generations of Kingsways had lived in the house until the last Kingsway died in 1974. After that, the house was sold to the present tenants, Lord and Lady Galloway.

Their daughter Katy (or Katherine, as Lady Galloway would always have addressed her with her full name) was born on the 12th of March 1978 When Katy was eighteen months old, Joel was born to Lady Galloway. Mrs Quigley, her housekeeper of over twenty years, had recently retired but had recommended a Scottish lady, Mrs Jane Walters, as a replacement. Even though Jane had a year-old son, Simon, Lady Galloway employed her. Katy and Joel, of course, were the children of 'The Old House', while Simon was just the housekeeper's son but at no time was he ever looked down on; rather, he was considered as a third child of the family.

Jane Walters, her husband James and son Simon lived in Douglas, the island's capital, where James worked as an estate agent. Jane's employment with Lady Galloway, however, was as a live-in housekeeper, so Jane and Simon moved north to reside at the Kingsway Mansion. Her days off, she of course spent with her husband in Douglas. As time passed, Jane noticed him becoming withdrawn. Although, when she asked if something was troubling him, James wouldn't tell her anything.

In the summer of 1979, James Walters mysteriously disappeared. After several unfruitful searches, Jane's hopes of tracing him vanished. Shaken by the disappearance of her husband and the seemingly endless accompanying police questioning, Jane felt she could no longer remain on the Isle of Man. She handed in her notice to Lady Galloway and shortly afterwards, left the island with her son and moved to Peebles in Scotland, where her family lived.

The letter arrived just six months into their life in Peebles. It was from Lady Galloway, asking Jane to consider returning to the Island to take up her old role as the housekeeper in the Kingsway Mansion. She said that a replacement just couldn't be found and that the children missed her and Simon. Family life in Peebles was not all that Jane had hoped for; there were family tensions Jane did not want to become involved in. Although her memories from the Isle of Man still hurt, she saw this opportunity as a godsend. Within a week, Jane and Simon were back on the Isle of Man, and Jane had resumed her previous duties.

The children, Simon, Katy and Joel, grew up together in the old house, where they enjoyed each other's friendship. Life on the Isle of Man was wonderful. School – great! The holidays – even better.

Chapter 2 – Simon

At school, Simon had found studying to be easy and enjoyable, so it was no surprise when he received top marks in all his tests and sailed through his A levels with high grades. Engineering was his goal and Edinburgh the university of choice. He remembered there were tears in his eyes when, in September 1996, Simon left his beloved island to begin studying at the University of Edinburgh. During the years that followed, letters were exchanged between Scotland and the Isle of Man and, of course, holiday visits by Simon to the Isle of Man and occasionally by Katy and Jane to Edinburgh – Joel was always too busy.

During his second year at university, Simon decided to join the Christian Union. As a child, he had attended Sunday school and a midweek Bible club held in the home of a school friend. His friend's mother, a devout Christian, taught Bible lessons, which Simon enjoyed very much. Although his Bible knowledge was a great asset at the Christian Union, it became evident to Simon that his knowledge of Scripture was not enough. He felt compelled to take the important step laid down in Scripture. Therefore, during the spring term, he accepted Jesus Christ as his Lord and Saviour and began attending Craiglockhart Community Church, where he was eventually baptised. Graham Dinsmore, the pastor, had attended the same Bible College as Simon; indeed, they had met in the Christian Union there, and it was Graham who led Simon to Christ. Even though he continued his engineering course and enjoyed it, Simon's heart was now set on a career in Christian ministry.

Craiglockhart Church, a fellowship with a growing congregation, was situated on the Craiglockhart Road, on the outskirts of Edinburgh. The congregation had a mix of labourers, hospital workers, students and business people. During Simon's second year at Bible College, the elders of Craiglockhart Community Church approached him to join their leadership team. The following year, his studies completed, the church leadership invited Simon to consider accepting the role of assistant pastor; it didn't take him long to accept.

Graham met with Simon and gave him a copy of his job description. Counselling would be a big part of his ministerial role – to college students struggling with workloads and exams, the unemployed and those with financial and family troubles. With some preaching also involved, the experience would prove invaluable in training Simon for his future ministry.

* * * *

In June 1999, Simon's mum Jane, accompanied by Katy and Joel, attended his graduation. Both during and following the ceremony, Jane and Katy took lots of photos of Simon in his hired gown. Jane then insisted on a restaurant meal before flying back on the evening plane. The meal was delicious, and the chat warm and informative, especially about the future of Katy and Joel.

Katy, having obtained a degree through the Open University, had applied and been accepted to Leicester

University to study for a master's degree in 'The Development Education Strategies of the Western Isles and Isle of Man.' Joel was living at home and looking for work, having completed his studies at the Further College in Douglas. His future, he had decided, was in politics.

When Simon's turn came to impart information, he told his mum and friends that he had applied and been accepted to Bible College in Glasgow to take a three-year theological degree course leading into the Christian ministry.

All too soon, the time came for the visitors to leave. Simon phoned for a taxi and, after hugs and goodbyes, the trio were on their way to the airport to head back to the Isle of Man.

In September 1999, Simon began his theological studies at Glasgow Bible College. The following years of study and practical work – and the church connections he made – convinced Simon that God had planned all of this in preparation for his future Christian service, wherever and whatever that would be.

Chapter 3 - Katy

In June 2000, half way through her master's degree, Katy was glad to return and spend summer on the Isle of Man and in 'The Old House'. She had obtained a part-time job at the Ramsey library and enjoyed helping Jane with the housework and cooking. She also enjoyed spending time again with Joel. One Friday evening he told her about his row with his dad over his association with David Kingston but assured her that he had broken with him although Kingston had ushered threats. But, Joel went on to assure her, he had something 'up his sleeve' to protect him from Kingston's threats. Troubled by some of what she heard, Katy decided to speak to her father.

'Joel told me he had broken off his relationship with David Kingston,' she informed him, 'But was concerned there might be repercussions.'

'He said, however,' Katy continued, 'that he had a means of securing his safety hidden away but wouldn't say where.'

'Joel told me that he and David Kingston had gone their separate ways,' responded her father. He paused, then continued: 'Look, I have some business to attend to tomorrow morning and Joel told me he is making a start on dismantling the horse boxes in the stables. He has some idea about converting the area into a games room, so I encouraged him. I will have a talk with him tomorrow afternoon. You go on to bed sweetheart and don't worry; leave it with me.'

On the following Saturday afternoon, after helping Jane prepare lunch, Katy went to the Kingsway stables to call Joel, and she found him hanging by his neck from a beam. For a moment she stared at the sight with her mouth hanging open, and then she screamed.

Jane, who was in the kitchen at the time, and Lord and Lady Galloway, discussing the dinner menu in the snug, heard her scream. All three rushed from the house to the stables. Lady Galloway collapsed at the sight. As Jane attended to her, Lord Galloway ran to Joel. Placing an upturned crate on its side, he climbed to cut the rope. He sliced through using his penknife, which he always carried with him. Katy, recovering from her initial shock, left to phone the police and an ambulance. As they waited for the police and ambulance to arrive, Katy shared her feelings with her father that somehow Joel's association with David Kingston had something to do with this tragedy. The mention of the name David Kingston made Lord Galloway grimace in anger. He had been warned about Joel's association with David Kingston by his friend the Chief Constable during one of their frequent games of chess. Just then the sound of the ambulance and police car arriving interrupted their conversation. Lord Galloway accompanied his wife to the hospital, leaving Katy and Jane to talk to the police.

Although no note accompanied Joel's body, the police determined it was suicide. At the inquest which followed shortly after the post mortem, the coroner agreed with the pathologist's findings and the police report. The verdict: Joel Galloway had taken his own life. In the hospital, Lady Galloway suffered a massive stroke and died. Broken hearted, at the loss of her Mum and her brother in such a brief period, Katy had been granted compassionate leave from Leicester University. With the release of her brother's body, she and her father planned for both funerals to take place at the same time.

Simon flew to the island for the funerals. He remarked to his mum that Lord Galloway looked so frail. His visit was brief, so he was unable to spend much time with Katy.

Despite the tragedy and trauma, Lord Galloway insisted that Katy leave and continue her studies for her master's. She did so, but with a heavy heart. Catching up with what she had missed helped her cope and soon she was settled once again into university life. Sharing a flat with two other students also helped immensely, especially when Katy discovered they were both churchgoers.

* * * *

In June 2003, just days after Katy returned home, her master's degree and graduation complete, Lord Galloway became ill. Jane and she were by his bedside when he died. Katy asked Jane to ring and tell Simon.

Once again Simon travelled to the Isle of Man for a funeral. Katy asked him to speak at the church service and pray at the graveside, and for this, Simon felt privileged. The Ramsey church building soon filled with neighbourhood folks and dignitaries. Adrian Porterhouse, the church pastor, conducted the service during which a few members of Tynwald, the Isle of Man's parliament in which Lord Galloway had served, paid tributes to their former colleague. In his closing message, Simon also paid tribute to his surrogate father and family. He took the opportunity to speak about Lord Galloway's faith in Christ and to assure the congregation that Katy hadn't lost her father; she knew where he was – 'with Christ, which was far better'.

After the funeral and customary refreshments, Simon managed to spend a considerable amount of time with Katy. He heard about her studies with the Open University and her time at Leicester University. He learned of her dad's generous financial support and how she had supplemented her fees by working in the Northern Hotel. As Katy spoke of her dad, tears began to flow. Then, during a period of grief counselling, Simon had another privilege; he led his childhood friend to faith in Christ.

Shortly afterwards, Katy said goodnight and retired to her bedroom. She opened the middle drawer of her dressing table and from it withdrew a brightly coloured box decorated with birds and flowers. She smiled as she remembered learning to decoupage as a teenager, and Caroline, one of her school friends, who had taught her the art. From the box, Katy took out two framed photographs: one of her mum and the other of her dad. Her eyes filled with tears as she regarded them lovingly. Another larger picture lay in the drawer, and as she lifted it out, her heart swelled with pride. This was a picture taken on the day her dad had been appointed to the House of Lords. Another photo emerged, taken on a very auspicious and atypical occasion when her father had become a member of the House of Keys.

Memories flooded back to her of school days when her teacher, Miss Quane, taught the class with pride and instilled in Katy a love of the Isle of Man and its history. Born and bred in Laxey, Miss Quane had taught in the small school there for many years before moving to Andreas in 1959. Katy remembered her first day at school in 1981. Miss Quane had favoured her, after all her father had not only been a member of the House of Keys, but the renowned Lord Galloway!

Katy brought out more paraphernalia, relating to the Isle of Man's government, its history and the foundation of Tynwald. She hadn't meant to, but she found herself voraciously reading through it. Katy found it all fascinating; indeed, it brought back memories of her thesis, written for her master's degree - 'The Development Strategies of the Western Isles and Isle of Man.' Halfway through reading the copious notes on Tynwald, dating back to Viking times, and the Isle of Man's history, modern and Celtic, her drooping eyelids won, and she fell asleep.

Katy awoke to glorious sunshine streaming in through her partially closed curtains. As she lay in bed, she made a decision; she would stay on the island for at least for a year or two, continue her part time job and consider her future and the future of Kingsway Mansion.

After showering and dressing, Katy joined Simon and Jane for breakfast.

Jane said, 'I wasn't going to wake you, dear, because I thought you might need some extra sleep. But I must say that you look quite refreshed!'

After their breakfast of tea, toast and poached eggs, Jane ordered Katy and Simon out of the kitchen, so she could wash the dishes.

The friends strolled through the morning sunshine and chatted about fun times in the old house.

Katy said, 'I have decided to stay at home and look for full-time employment, perhaps a teaching post. I need to put my master's degree to some use. What about you? What are your plans?'

'I am enjoying my work with the Craiglockhart Church, but I'm not sure where my future lies. I might go back to college and study for a BA.'

They chatted some more until Jane called them in for coffee and gave Katy a letter which had just arrived. Simon, having already packed, said goodbye to Katy and assured her he would keep in touch.

After Jane left to drive Simon to the airport, Katy opened the letter and read its contents:

'My dear Miss Galloway, please accept my sympathy on the death of your brother, but he had a document of mine which I urgently need. Please search for it and let me know when you find it. You will recognise it by the name IOM Property Company at the top. Ring me on this number.'

The message wasn't signed but included a mobile number, so she rang the number. The call went immediately to voicemail. Katy left a message asking for more details and, somewhat reluctantly, gave her mobile number.

Chapter 4 - Application

Katy was puzzled. She had gathered Joel's things all together and found nothing with the words IOM Property Company. Putting the letter in her desk drawer, Katy picked up the morning newspaper and read through the situations vacant column. She saw an advertisement entered by the Education Authority, stating that Douglas High School required a history teacher for the new term. She thought about what she had said to Simon earlier about a teaching post and offered up a silent prayer of thanksgiving. The advert also stated that Thursday, which was the following day, was the last day for applications.

Katy immediately telephoned the number supplied, gave her name to the Secretary of the Department of Education and requested an application form. The secretary introduced herself as Karen Burrell, a fellow student from high school. Katy vaguely remembered that Karen had been a few years above her at school.

Karen apologised and told Katy that no more application forms were to be sent out.

'Try ringing Mrs Groves, the school principal. You will know her better as our former teacher, Miss Freeman. She is the one who rang earlier this morning to request that no more application forms be sent out.'

Katy thanked her and said she would call into the school. They chatted for a while longer until the ringing of Katy's mobile ended their conversation. Katy answered her phone and discovered that Jane was calling to explain she had some shopping to do at Tynwald Mills and would stay in Tynwald for lunch.

Tynwald Mills, Katy recalled, was her mum's favourite shopping place. It was so called because it was close to the famous Tynwald Hill, the traditional ancient meeting place of the Manx parliamentary assembly. Once again Katy's eyes filled with tears as she remembered the picnics on the Manx National Day, the 5th of July. Each year on that day, hundreds would gather to watch the governmental processions. Joel and she would look along the parading ranks and wave when dad appeared wearing his regalia. He, of course, never waved back.

Katy looked at her watch: 10.30 a.m. It seemed ages since breakfast. Suddenly the house appeared to close in on her; Katy shuddered and phoned Jane to say she would join her for lunch. During lunch, Katy asked Jane to consider staying on in Kingsway Mansion.

'I would still need help looking after the house and I would miss your company,' she admitted.

Jane smiled, hugged her, and said she would be delighted to stay.

'After all it has been my home for so many years, thank you. Now I have some friends I want to visit so I'll see you later – at home!'

That afternoon, Katy knocked on the principal's office door.

The principal, Mrs Groves, looked at her visitor and exclaimed, 'Well, bless my soul, if it isn't Katy Galloway!'

Katy greeted her and explained why she was calling.

Mrs Groves confessed she had been expecting her as Karen had phoned the school after Katy's earlier phone call. She told Katy she was sorry to hear about her dad.

'You know,' Mrs Groves said in a sad voice, 'I asked him to speak on the history of the Isle of Man at the Ladies' Guild open evening. He agreed and called to see me at my home to discuss the programme.'

With a sigh, she added, 'That was just a week before your father's death.'

Her face then brightened as she continued, 'Your father spoke very highly of you, Katy. He was always telling people about your achievements at Leicester University. Anyway, when I heard that he had taken ill, I decided that I should speak at the Guild meeting myself.'

Mrs Groves went on. 'And by the way, no one else who applied has your qualifications.'

She then handed Katy an application form, 'You will, however, need to complete this. Oh, and while I'm buttering you up,' she added with a smile, 'would you take next week's guild meeting on the island's history? You will do it so much better than I.'

Katy smiled in return, 'How can I say no? Send me a text with any details I might need to know; my mobile number will be on the application form.'

The following Wednesday evening, dressed in her Sunday best, Katy drove to the Church of England church hall in Douglas.

She arrived early and set up her laptop and projector. She was glad to see the wall at the rear of the platform had been painted white, as it would serve as a screen. As the hall gradually filled, Katy was pleased to see a few familiar faces.

Mrs Groves introduced her as the guest speaker and again offered her condolences on the deaths of her parents. She also spoke highly of Katy's mother and said that it had been a privilege to have had Lady Galloway as a member of the Guild. Following a hymn and the Guild formalities, during which she introduced Katy's topic, Mrs Groves handed over the platform to Katy.

'Good afternoon,' said Katy, 'My subject is one close to my heart, thanks mainly to two people: my former primary school teacher, the late Miss Quane, and your chairperson, Mrs Groves, who both instilled in me a love of the Isle of Man and its history. Some of what I have to say may be familiar to you, but I know from experience that not everyone who lives in the Isle of Man is acquainted with its roots.'

Katy pressed the button on her remote control, and a picture of the British Isles appeared on the screen.

'The Isle of Man, known affectionately as *'the jewel in the Irish Sea'*, lies midway between Ireland and the North of England. It is approximately 32 miles long and about 15 miles wide. The capital is Douglas, and in 1994, the island had a population of around 75,000. The indigenous inhabitants were known as Manx, and their name for the island was *Ellan Vannin*, also known simply as *Mann*. It is a self-governing Crown dependency, although the head of state is Queen Elizabeth II, who holds the title of *Lord of Mann*. The Lord of Mann is represented by a Lieutenant Governor, although foreign relations and defence are the responsibility of the British Government.'

Katy paused, looked around her audience and smiled, 'That was just for anyone here who is perhaps new to the island. Now for the serious bit.' With words and projected pictures, Katy took her audience on a journey through the three periods of the history: the Celtic period, the Scandinavian rule and, finally, the British oversight. 'Remember that, although the Isle of Man is classified as a British isle, it is not part of the United Kingdom.' She concluded by outlining the facts concerning the island's government.

On completion of her presentation, the Guild members responded with a resounding applause. Mrs Groves congratulated Katy on a splendid talk; she seemed especially taken with the pictures. During the refreshments that followed, Katy received more compliments. Mrs Hanna, the chairperson, and Miss Corlett, a member of the school board, remarked on the professionalism of her presentation. The former asked her to come in on Monday morning to meet with the other members of the school board regarding her recent application.

Chapter 5 - Vocation

On Monday morning, Mrs Hanna opened the interview by asking Katy some questions about her experience. Katy explained that her qualifications included an Open University degree and her master's degree. Only two other board members spoke and both asked questions about her family. The chairperson concluded the interview by telling the board members about Katy's presentation at the Guild. She then asked Katy to wait for them in the corridor. Five minutes later, the board called Katy back into the room and told her that the members unanimously agreed she was the applicant best suited for the position of a history teacher. Mrs Groves suggested that they meet the following morning and discuss starting times and salary.

On Tuesday morning, Mrs Groves met with Katy and outlined the salary structure, job description and school policies. She gave Katy written documentation to read over before making a decision.

Katy, her heart pounding with excitement, just smiled and thanked Mrs Groves.

'My decision is already made,' she said with a grin, 'I will accept the position.'

'Perfect!' the delighted principal exclaimed. 'Can you start on Monday morning?'

For Katy, the next two years were marvellous, as she enjoyed teaching her favourite subject. Holidays were spent either in Scotland with Jane and Simon—who had returned to college to study for a BA degree—or with Simon on the Isle of Man.

During her first school year Katy led the afterschool Scripture Union (SU). The school's SU committee, made up of senior students and Katy, met in her home once a month to discuss programmes and guest speakers. One day, Harold Monks was their guest speaker. He was the uncle of one of their newer members and the director of an African mission.

Harold Monk's talk on the African Missionary Society held the group's attention and generated many questions. Harold left some leaflets about the work of the mission. Katy gave a word of thanks and escorted him to the school gate. After saying goodbye, Katy returned to the SU meeting room and helped gather up the leaflets. The students never hung around; instead, they disappeared quickly as soon as each meeting ended. She sat at a desk and read through one of the leaflets.

Later that evening at home, Katy called Mr Monk and said she would like to speak to him about the short-term work listed in his leaflets. The conversation lasted for quite a while, during which time Katy arranged to visit the mission's headquarters in Sheffield. There, she could discuss the various mission projects and find out what ministry, if any, would suit her skills.

Later that day, Katy told Jane about her plans and that she had decided half-term would be the time to go.

* * * *

Then another mysterious letter arrived from the same property company. It stated that '*because the writer had not received the requested item, dire consequences would result'*. It also warned Katy *'to keep looking over her shoulder'*. Katy sat down and read the letter again. What item was the writer talking about? Her hand shaking, Katy put it in her desk drawer. She decided to do nothing about the letters until after she returned from Sheffield.

Katy's visit to Sheffield was very productive. At the headquarters of the African Mission Society, she learned more about their programme and enquired about a short-term involvement over the summer. The UK Director, Mr Len Raines, was delighted with Katy's request; plans were put in place for a trip to Zambia during the summer of 2005.

Excited, Katy arrived back on the Isle of Man and soon shared her visit with Jane. Jane said that she was pleased and, she added, so would Simon be when she told him.

Jane then told Katy the news about Simon's future.

'Now he has his BA degree, Craiglockhart Church leadership want him back as an associate pastor to work alongside the lead pastor Graham who is now teaching part-time in Bible college.'

Katy gave her a searching look, 'Maybe you want to pay Simon a visit?'

Jane smiled back at her and said, 'Perhaps I might.' Then, wistfully she added, 'I wish you were free to come with me.'

'So do I,' replied Katy, 'but I have too much to do here.'

The following week, Katy drove Jane to the airport and waved her off on the early morning flight to

Glasgow. She felt a sinking feeling in her stomach; she would have longed to accompany her to see Simon.

Katy had not shared the letters with Jane but that evening after school, she took them from the desk drawer and read them again. Filled with dread she again searched Joel's room but found nothing. Frantic now with worry, Katy phoned the police station but replaced the receiver before anyone answered.

'No,' she said to herself, 'I'll talk things over with Jane when she returns.'

Chapter 6 – Danger

On Jane's return, Katy showed her the letters and said she had decided to move to Douglas and find someone to rent Kingsway Mansion.

'After all, that is where I work, and this place is too big for me to live in. I'll place an advert in the local papers and I suppose it should be sooner rather than later,' said Katy, pulling a wry face. 'I hope I'm doing the right thing; I don't want to leave you homeless.'

'Well,' responded Jane, 'that's the least of your worries. Let's pray about it.'

They proceeded to do just that.

As Katy worked in the kitchen the following Saturday morning, a car entered the driveway. The occupant did not alight, but a face hidden by a Margaret Thatcher mask appeared at the window. The wearer wagged a finger in Katy's direction before opening the door and throwing something on the drive. By the time Katy opened the front door, the car had gone. Gingerly, Katy walked towards the item lying on the gravel. Jane shouted out not to touch it and phoned the police. After her phone call, during which Jane explained what had occurred, they both drank coffee and waited for the police.

Jane and Katy were surprised when a police car arrived followed by an army vehicle. An army officer alighted and asked the police to reverse their car to a safe distance. He walked towards the object and peered at it closely. He then signalled to the other occupant of the army truck. A soldier appeared and lowered a ramp at the rear of the vehicle, then he stood back and manoeuvred something in his hand. When a small robot on caterpillar tracks came slowly into view, Jane and Katy knew what would happen next. They had seen such a bomb disposal robot at work on television during the Northern Ireland 'Troubles'. The army officer then spoke to Katy and Jane and suggested they move to the rear of the house.

Operated by remote control, the robot moved towards what the officer hoped was not a bomb. The robot's mechanical arm reached out, and when it touched the object, there came a loud pop! The package flew open, and the robot went into reverse. The army officer walked over and looked down. He then picked up the remains of the package and walked towards the house. The two ladies answered his knock.

'I'm afraid this is someone's idea of a sick joke,' he said, holding out a sheet of card with the word BOOM printed on it. 'The perpetrator fitted it with a kind of miniature firework-type device, well, that's the simplest explanation. It's operated by movement—clever, but dangerous. There is a scorch mark on the robot's arm. If you had touched it, your hand would have received a severe burn. I'll take the item with me, and the police will have some questions, I'm sure. Good day.'

After he had walked away, two policemen approached the house and Katy invited them in. As they talked, the army vehicle drove away. Katy decided to show the policemen the letters she had received. One of the officers took them to show the Chief Constable.

Somehow the incident didn't reach the press, which Katy said was God's doing. However, she did put a notice in the newspaper the next day declaring that: 'Katy Galloway no longer resides at Kingsway Mansion, Andreas. Please address all mail to Box No. 325 at the Isle of Man post office.' She also purchased a new SIM card for her mobile phone and texted all her contacts with the new number.

Before going to school the following morning, Katy called to visit a lady who had been a friend of her mother. Mrs March lived in Onchan, a village on the outskirts of Douglas. Katy still had time for a cup of tea before work, so as they supped, she asked if Mrs March had ever considered taking in a lodger.

With a slightly puzzled expression on her face, Mrs March asked, 'Who did you have in mind?'

Katy replied, 'Me!'

The puzzled expression was replaced by one of genuine surprise. 'But, what about your home?'

'I am now working in Douglas, so I feel I should live here,' Katy explained. 'I want to rent out Kingsway Mansion. At present, Jane Walters is living there with me. You remember Jane?'

'Of course I do!' replied Mrs March in a mock gruff voice, 'Ask her to call and see me sometime.' After Katy's nod of agreement, she added, 'And, if you wish, you can lodge with me. I'd be delighted with the company.'

'I know Miss Wilson visits you,' Katy said, 'I teach with her. She says you play Scrabble together. Well, I can make a threesome!'

At this, they both laughed, and Katy left for school.

Later on, at break time, Katy sought out Miss Wilson and told her what she had decided regarding lodgings.

In the weeks to follow, Katy and Eileen Wilson became good friends. Although Eileen was at least twenty years older than she was (or so Katy surmised), they found they had some common interests. Miss Wilson confided in Katy that she had decided to take early retirement at the end of term and go back to her old haunts in Donegal. She had a sister who lived there and who was not keeping well and needed someone to take care of her.

Katy placed advertisements in all of the town's newspapers and within a week she had four responses. She chose a family from Douglas who agreed to rent Kingsway Mansion for at least a year. Katy didn't mention the 'bomb'; she felt assured that no more threats would come to the house.

Katy had chosen a house agent in Ramsey to look after the house in her absence and provided him with two keys. She gave the tenants his address and phone number then locked up her home. Standing by her packed car, Katy gave Kingsway Mansion a long, sad look then drove to Onchan.

Chapter 7 - Changes

Simon had rented a small flat in Lanark Road, but during his mum's visit, she had insisted on staying in a nearby hotel. They both ate dinner there most evenings; Simon remarked that it was like being on holiday.

Arriving back from work one evening, Simon found a letter from his mum, explaining that she was no longer employed at Kingsway Mansion and that Katy had decided to rent the house to a local family and move to Douglas. Jane also wrote that, in his will, Lord Galloway had left her a substantial sum of money, and she felt very much inclined to retire to Scotland – not to Peebles, but to Marchmont, Edinburgh, where she had already purchased an apartment.

Simon knew from preaching in that district of Edinburgh that Marchmont was an affluent area in the south of the capital, just fifteen minutes from Princess Street. Marchmont had been developed as a planned, middle-class tenement suburb in the nineteenth century. The area had a blend of Victorian and Edwardian buildings characterised by their tall ceilings and spacious rooms with fine period features, including original fireplaces, cornicing and wooden floors. Apartments in Marchmont were very attractive and highly sought after by both professionals and students. It was one of these typical but unfurnished apartments that Jane had bought. She never did tell him how much Lord Galloway had left her in his will, and Simon never asked.

Later that evening Simon received an email from a former Bible College friend, Kenneth Craig. Kenneth and he had shared a flat during their Bible College years and they had kept in touch. In the email, Kenneth explained that he was on furlough from his mission in Africa and staying for eighteen months. He planned to be in Edinburgh the following Wednesday and suggested meeting up. Simon replied suggesting they meet at Waverly train station at two o'clock.

They met as planned, but Kenneth apologised; he hadn't long to stay because his mission secretary had arranged a last-minute deputation meeting in Falkirk. They spent a pleasant two hours drinking coffee, reminiscing, and laughing at memories of fun times in college. Simon also learned of Kenneth's involvement in Uganda with Mission to Africa, an organisation he had applied to work with during his last few months at Bible College. All too soon, the time came for Kenneth to leave and catch the train to Falkirk. They promised to keep in touch, but somehow, never did; many years would pass before the two would meet again.

* * * *

Jane flew to Glasgow at the end of May 2004, and Simon met her at the airport. Edinburgh and the apartment were their main topics of conversation, but Katy and Kingsway were a close second. Jane sent Katy pictures of the apartment and invited her to come and stay during the summer. Two days later Katy phoned.

'Hi Jane,' she said, 'lovely apartment. I wonder, with the school closed for the Tourist Trophy races (TT) as it's located on the race course, would now suit for a visit?'

'You would be most welcome,' Jane exclaimed, 'I'm missing you already!'

The next day, Jane picked Katy up from Glasgow airport. Jane had phoned to tell Simon of Katy's plans, and he said he would call when she arrived. Katy took her case to the Marchmont apartment's second bedroom, which had been prepared for her stay.

Katy told Jane that she had received an invitation from the African mission to work on a short-term project in Zambia during July of next year.

'As you know,' said Katy, 'the school term in the Isle of Man doesn't finish until the end of July but Mrs Groves has given me permission to accept the mission trip and, when I return, to use it as a means of widening my class' experience. I wrote and accepted the offer; I leave at the end of June just before the Zambian school half-term. July is winter there, so I've been told to bring warm clothes for day and night. The local mission director is a lady called Jennifer with whom I have already been in touch; she will meet me at the airport. Isn't it exciting?'

Smiling at Katy's enthusiasm, Jane concurred.

Simon arrived for supper and Jane, Simon and Katy talked well into the night. By the time Simon left to drive the short distance to his flat, he and Jane had learned of Joel's dubious friendships, Katy's shock, and her feelings on finding her brother in the stable. She had her suspicions about his death. Firstly, there had been no suicide note, and secondly, during her conversation with Joel on Friday evening, he'd been excited when telling her of his plans. Joel had also told her, touching the side of his nose in that secretive way, there were things he knew that would help him climb the ladder of success.

She remembered hearing a conversation between her father and the Chief Constable, who often visited their home. He and Lord Galloway had been ardent chess players who'd enjoyed playing each other. She was passing the open door of the room her father called his snug when she heard Joel's name mentioned. Katy stopped to listen. The Chief Constable was voicing his concern about the company Joel was keeping, and she heard him mention an especially dubious businessman named David Kingston who was suspected by the police of very shady business deals. They were keeping him under surveillance, but he was a slippery customer; so far, they did not have enough evidence to make an arrest. Joel was often seen in his company, so it was thought that he might be a messenger or a go-between. The Chief Constable urged her father to speak with Joel. Just then, Katy heard her mother approaching, so she hurried off to her room.

She remembered seeing Joel with a man who could have been David Kingston. The next evening, she was told about the blazing row during which Joel had shouted at his father to mind his own business and stop trying to interfere in his career. He had then stormed out of the house. The following day, Friday, Joel returned and apologized to his father, assuring him that he had no need to worry and that he, Joel, was sorting out a company problem. Later, Joel had knocked on Katy's bedroom door, and they talked about his future. He gave very little away but assured Katy that things were looking up for him. When she asked about David Kingston, he told her that it was probably Kingston she saw him with in Douglas, but he had severed all contacts with that man. He left Katy at 10.00 p.m. on that Friday evening, and at Saturday lunchtime, she found Joel hanging in the stable.

'The date,' Katy said, 'is etched in my memory: the 26th of August 2000.'

Katy stayed a few more days during which she spent most of her time with Simon.

Back on the Isle of Man, TT over, Katy returned and resumed the summer term but found concentration difficult and was pleased when the end of June came, and she began her pre-arranged holiday. Mrs March assured Katy that her room would be still there for her when she returned. Packed and ready, Katy caught her flights, first to Manchester, then on to Zambia.

Chapter 8– Zambia

Excited and expectant, Katy arrived for her first mission in Zambia. Jennifer, with whom she'd had quite a lot of correspondence over the past few weeks, greeted her at the Lusaka International Airport. As Jennifer drove the fifteen or so kilometres to the African Missionary Society office, they chatted about Katy's initial role with the mission. To Katy's surprise, Jennifer was the only full-time employee in Lusaka. Over coffee at the office, though, Jennifer explained that there were volunteer helpers. Later, Katy was introduced to Kitana, who helped with office work, and Elida, the caretaker. Both were local ladies who voluntarily gave of their time.

Jennifer explained that she too had lived most of her life in Zambia, having been born there. But she'd studied for a time in Boston, USA, before joining the mission. She then told Katy that the mission had obtained lodgings for her with an English lady, Mrs Buxton, and they would go round there once they had eaten.

'I know a popular café nearby which does excellent dinners,' she said.

Later that evening, Katy was introduced to Mrs Buxton and her room. Mrs Buxton explained that breakfast was between eight and nine o'clock and though she didn't 'do' dinners she could provide supper.

The two weeks flew by during which Katy accompanied Jennifer throughout Zambia. They visited mission supporters and schools. Katy also received an invitation to share something of life on the Isle of Man at Jennifer's church.

During her stay, Katy learned that Mrs Buxton was from Bristol. Her late husband had worked with an engineering company in Zambia and when he died she decided to stay and open her home as a guest house.

When the time came for Katy to leave Zambia and return to the Isle of Man, Jennifer drove her to the airport where they hugged and said goodbye. As Katy's plane took off, she closed her eyes, her mind full of so many precious memories.

* * * *

Back on the Isle of Man, Katy took a taxi to Mrs March's house. Already the leaves on the trees were changing colour; autumn was on its way. Katy returned to school on the 1st of September and though she still enjoyed teaching her class, she felt unsettled. Each night she sought the Lord for guidance regarding her future.

One morning in mid-September she opened her Bible and read about the storm on the sea of Galilee. Her Bible notes were based on the storm, Jesus walking on the water and Peter stepping out of the boat at Jesus' command. The closing challenge was: 'If you don't step out of the boat, you'll never know if you can walk on water.' Katy decided she would 'step out of her boat'.

She wrote to the African Mission headquarters and applied for a further and longer period of service in Zambia. Within a week a letter arrived stating that the mission had received a glowing report from Jennifer and the missionary board had decided to forgo another interview. There was an opening for a worker in Zambia in November and a five-year period of mission. The position was with a school there and was hers if she wanted it, but she would have to provide her own financial support.

Katy accepted their offer, assured the board the finance was no problem and that she could leave in November.

An excited Katy wrote to Jane and told her of her plans and that she would keep in touch once settled in Zambia. Next, she handed in her resignation to the school board, effective at the end of October. Katy also wrote and shared her decision with her former school colleague Eileen Wilson, who, after her retirement, was living in Donegal, Ireland and with whom she had kept in touch.

On 23rd September 2005, Katy taught History of the Western Isles at school, which she loved, and then drove to Ramsey to see her agent who informed her that the tenants had given notice. Katy told him of her plan to go again to Africa for two years and paid him in advance regarding the house. When she said she needed to visit the house and collect some things for her journey, he told her the tenants were on holiday and gave her a key.

Once more a tinge of sadness filled her as she entered her home. A letter with familiar handwriting lay in the hallway. Katy read the enclosed note:

'Where are you, Miss Galloway? I drove to your house, but I didn't recognise the occupants. The lady said they were tenants and informed me that you were in Africa; what are you doing there? Did my 'bomb' scare you off? And where is my document? I am getting infuriated, and I will find you.'

Frowning, Katy put the letter into her handbag then went to her bedroom, which she had kept locked, and filled a

CHAPTER 8 – ZAMBIA

box with letters and books including her journal. Suddenly, in a blinding flash, a memory returned. When they were children, she and Joel had a secret hiding place in the stable in the unused glove compartment of a horse stall. Katy picked up her box of trivia and locked up the house, put the box in her car and walked to the stables. Katy soon found the secret place, and from the compartment, she withdrew three pieces of paper. Two she knew right away were the documents that her letter writer wanted, the other was a note in Joel's handwriting.

August 2001
Hi, Sis. By the time you read this, I will be in Africa. I am not telling you where because, when you tell Dad, he will likely want to send out a search party. (Here, Joel drew a small smiley face.) I have had a great offer from David Kingston to become a diplomatic courier. I will be travelling between Africa and England, carrying important messages, but I can't tell you to whom. I will send you letters, but they will be from an address in England. Tell Dad not to try and contact the family at this address; they are only go-betweens. I'll send my letters to England via their African relatives; they will know just to post them on. Look after yourself, Sis – maybe you'll marry Simon! (Another smiley face followed this).

Katy cried. She took the papers to her car and put them in her handbag, then drove back to her agent.

'I don't want to rent out my home again; I might sell the house when I return,' she said. 'If I contact an auctioneer, would you liaise with him or her regarding the house contents? Tell the auction house to take every-thing, sell what they can and give the rest to charity.'

'Tell you what,' said her agent, 'You go and make preparations your trip to Africa, and I will look after the auctioneering of your house contents. If you trust me with your bank details, I can deposit your earnings. I will lock up the house and keep an eye on it till you return.'

Katy assured him of her trust and gave him her bank details. With peace of mind and thoughts full of the forthcoming trip to Africa, she drove back to Onchan.

The following day, Saturday, Mrs March asked her to accompany her to the Tynwald Shopping Centre in St Johns. However, when Mrs March was looking else-where in the store, and Katy was buying a skirt and blouse at the counter, someone spoke her name. Katy turned to see a man smiling at her. He said she was a dif-ficult person to find. Somehow, Katy knew right away that this was the letter-writer, and her suspicions were confirmed when he added that he'd expected a phone call from her. All of a sudden, she realised she had seen this man with Joel in Douglas; it was David Kingston, the man she suspected of murdering Joel.

A feeling of dread came over her, and she began to scream and call for the police. The man left in a hurry and disappeared, pushing his way roughly through the gathering crowd. The manager of the shopping centre arrived and lead Katy to his office when Mrs March turned up. She had seen what happened and hurried over to be with her. Katy apologised and asked him not to call the police and said it was a misunderstanding. As Katy and Mrs March left the centre, it started to rain, and Katy was glad of an excuse to pull her coat hood up over her face. In the car, she apologised to Mrs March.

When they were safely back at Mrs March's house, Katy explained about the threatening letters and that she thought the man from the store was the letter-writer. That evening Katie telephoned her friend Miss Wilson in Donegal and asked if she could stay with her for a while. Miss Wilson asked no questions and said she would love to have company.

At break time the following Monday morning, Katy called into the principal's office. She told Mrs Groves about the threats and that she would like to leave as soon as possible. I want to put the island and the threats behind me. I will not leave a forwarding address for myself, but the school can use Mrs March's address; the office has it on file. And please, let me go quietly.'

'I have your resignation letter on file,' said Mrs Groves sadly, 'I'll find a substitute teacher and you can leave at the end of the week. I will square it with the school board and I am sure there will be no objections. Wages due will to go into your account.'

Katy left the office and continued as proposed. The board agreed to her leaving early and on Friday afternoon Katy presented herself at the principal's office once again.

To her surprise, Mrs Hanna, the chairperson of the board was there.

'I felt I couldn't let you leave without saying goodbye,' she said, 'and to tell you that the school board has decided to pay you up until the end of October. We hope it will help towards your missionary trip.'

'That is very generous,' responded Katy, 'and it will help with the financing of my time in Africa. Thank you.'

Mrs Groves handed over the necessary job leaving documentation, they all shook hands, and Katy left the school wondering if she would ever be back.

Katy then called in at the police station and was recognised by the Sergeant from the 'bomb' episode. She
related the incident at Tynwald and gave him the letter
she found at her house. Katy told him that she was
leaving the island and would not return for at least two
years. The Sergeant assured her he would pass the letter
on but the mobile number from one of the other letters
was no longer in use.

* * * *

Now unemployed, Katy was sitting reading in Mrs
March's parlour when her mobile rang. It was her agent
to say that the auctioneers were available on Saturday
morning to take away the house contents and wondered, knowing she was still on the Isle of Man, if Katy
would like to be there.

Katy decided she would but told him to oversee
everything as planned. She then decided to phone Mrs
Wilson to ask if she could come to Donegal right away;
a request to which Eileen Wilson gave a resounding yes.
Katy then booked a one-way ticket on the 7 p.m.
Saturday night boat to Dublin.

Mrs March was in Peel visiting friends and staying
for the weekend. She didn't own a mobile phone, so
Katy left her a note explaining that for personal reasons
she had decided to leave the Isle of Man immediately
and would get in touch with her from Zambia. Katy left
a cheque to cover her month's lodgings then packed up
all her belongings.

Katy then remembered the last letter received from
the man she believed to be David Kingston. He may or
may not have seen Mrs March in the Tynwald Centre,
but Katy decided to make sure that her landlady was in

no danger from this man that she believed had some-thing to do with her brother's death.

The following morning Katy drove to her old home once again, her car packed with everything she would need for Donegal and Africa. The auctioneers' vans and her agent were already there. Once the men had every-thing taken from her home, Katy waved them off and strolled around the house and grounds. Even then she still felt constrained to sell her old home with all its memories. Just then her mobile rang; it was her agent asking if she had a key. Just after answering yes, Katy heard a rattling sound from the snug room. She rushed in and found a small bird fluttering around close to the window. Placing her phone on the windowsill, she opened the window and tried to shoo the bird out, but it flew from the snug to the hall. Katy closed the window and ran after it. She made sure all other doors were closed and opened the front door. The little bird found its way of escape and left the house.

Katy followed the bird out and locked the front door. She climbed into her car and without a backwards glance, she drove away from Kingsway Mansion. She stopped in Ramsey and cancelled her PO Box. Katy then drove to Douglas where, after lunch, she spent most of the afternoon shopping. At the sea terminal bistro, she had a light tea and drove onto the Dublin ferry at 6 p.m.

Katy arrived late in Dublin and booked into a Premier Inn. She searched her pockets and car for her mobile phone, then realised she had switched it off in Kingsway and left it on the windowsill when rescuing the bird. The phone was secured with a password so no one else could use it but all her contacts were on it, so she couldn't ring anyone. She remembered some numbers were in her journal on the back page, including Miss Wilson's, but not the numbers for Simon or Jane. Next morning Katy visited a Vodafone shop and fixed herself up with a new mobile. She then rang Miss Wilson to say she would arrive with her in the afternoon and began her journey north.

Ireland was a land of oxymoron. Malin Head, the northernmost part of Ireland, was in the south. The island of Ireland had two separate states: Northern Ireland was part of the United Kingdom, whereas Southern Ireland was a republic. Donegal was part of the Republic of Ireland, and Malin Head was in Donegal.

Eileen Wilson lived just outside of Malin Town in a house formerly belonging to her deceased sister. Eileen's sister had left her home to Eileen in her will, and she had used it as a holiday home during the years she worked on the Isle of Man. Now retired she loved being back in her home territory. As Katy drove up to her friend's house, she thought how similar Donegal was to the Isle of Man. Eileen came out to greet Katy on her arrival late on that September evening. To the west, the Atlantic Ocean glowed red and gold and Katy could understand why Eileen loved it there. Together they emptied Katy's car and then settled down to supper and sunset.

Katy enjoyed her time with Eileen and the many trips with her throughout Inishowen, the name of the peninsula which contained the town of Malin. Katy also visited the ancient city of Derry and walked around the famous city walls.

Although she enjoyed her time with Eileen, she was glad when the time came to leave for Zambia. Her car had low mileage, and Katy sold it easily in Derry for a good price. During her stay, Katy booked her flight to

Zambia, flying from Dublin airport at 2 p.m. on 1st November 2005.

With Eileen's permission, she left quite a bit of her belongings with her, including the box of stuff from Kingsway. Katy did, however, take the Ayre documents—the papers she had retrieved from the stable—in her hand luggage. Eileen drove her to Letterkenny, one of Donegal's main towns, and to the bus station where Katy caught the bus for Dublin. Eileen hugged her goodbye, and soon Katy was on the first leg of her journey to Zambia.

Chapter 9 – Mr Equinox

During the twelve-and-a-half-hour flight, Katy read, ate and slept. Jennifer met her at the airport and drove her straight to Mrs Buxton's house where she was lodging.

'I will pick you up tomorrow at 9 a.m.,' said Jennifer, 'Enjoy your evening and have a good night's sleep.'

Mrs Buxton showed Katy to her room, a different one this time, and told her to come for supper when she was ready.

Katy began unpacking only to discover that not only had she left her former mobile in the Isle of Man, but she had also left her journal in Donegal. She wondered how she could get a message to Simon or Jane but shrugged her shoulders and decided to leave it to the very resourceful Simon to find a way of contacting her.

Katy did sleep well, and next morning she accompanied Jennifer on her rounds. The first stop was the local school, Lusaka Primary and Intermediate, founded by the mission in 1964; Jennifer had taught there for a time.

'The principal knows you are coming to help and he will explain your programme,' said Jennifer as they travelled.

She introduced Katy to the principal Mr Kabaghe who, over coffee, told Katy that she could visit two days each week and conduct several classes. Her responsibility would be to help the children improve their English. Although all of the children already spoke English, their native dialects of Bemba and Nyanja permeated their speech and writing.

As the days passed, Katy travelled with Jennifer to schools where she had agreed other teaching assignments. When she commenced her posts in these schools she fell in love with the Zambian children.

During the school half-term, Monday 3rd July to Friday 7th July, Jennifer and Katy flew to Botswana for a short hotel break. Katy remembered a little of Botswana from reading the *No. 1 Detective Agency,* books. Jennifer hired a car, and they managed to see quite a bit of the sparsely populated country. They visited the nature reserves and the markets; Katy especially loved the markets with their stalls and smells. They took plenty of photos.

One day during their holiday, the women were having coffee at their hotel café when Jennifer spotted an old school friend and excused herself to go and talk to her. It was then that a man approached Katy. She was startled to hear her name. Looking up, she saw a stranger standing by her table.

'Well, well, if it isn't Katy Galloway, far from her home on the Isle of Man,' the stranger said in a sneering manner, 'You won't know me, but I know you.'

'Who are you?' asked a suddenly frightened Katy, 'And how do you know my name?'

'You can call me Mr Equinox,' the man replied, 'And I have known you for many years.'

'Do you know me from the Isle of Man?' asked Katy.

'Enough questions,' he answered, 'I want your camera.'

'Why?' asked Katy.

'I recognised you when I saw you at the market in Botswana, you and your friend were taking photographs' explained Mr Equinox, 'And I think I might be in one of them.' His tone grew threatening: 'I don't like having my picture taken. So, camera please.'

Frightened and not knowing what to say or do, Katy obeyed. She reached into her bag and produced her camera. The stranger opened the battery compartment and removed the memory card.

Just then, Jennifer returned, accompanied by a gentleman:

'Excuse me, sir,' he said, addressing the man at Katy's table, 'I am the manager of this café. This young lady thinks you are threatening her friend.'

'Not at all,' responded the so-called Mr Equinox, 'I know Katy from of old.'

Handing her back her camera, he smiled at her and said, 'I'll be in touch.'

Before Katy could reply, the man strolled away.

'Are you all right, miss?' asked the manager, 'Your friend observed you from the terrace and came and fetched me. We both observed the frightened expression on your face as the man took your camera.'

Jennifer looked at Katy and said, 'Hey, I brought you on holiday to put some colour in your face, but you look as if you have seen a ghost! Who was that man? And why did he want your camera?'

'He called himself Mr Equinox. He said he didn't like having his picture taken; he opened the camera and took my memory card.'

'But, Katy,' said Jennifer, 'Don't you remember? Your battery went flat in the early part of our trip.'

Then Jennifer exclaimed, 'Oh, you did take a picture, but with my camera! We were at a market in Francistown, and you took a picture of me, displaying some beads I had bought. Perhaps your Mr Equinox was in the background and saw you taking the picture?'

'But he knew me,' said Katy, 'He said he'd known me for a long time. He wouldn't answer when I asked him how he knew me though.'

Suddenly, Jennifer, too, was frightened, 'When Mr Equinox discovers that it wasn't your camera, he will be back looking for me. Somehow, I think our holiday is over.'

With that, the women made their way back to the hotel, occasionally glancing over their shoulders. But Katy saw no sign of Mr Equinox. Once in their room, Jennifer went on the Internet and changed their return flight to Zambia. That evening, with sighs of relief, they were airborne, saying goodbye to Botswana and, hopefully, Mr Equinox.

* * * *

Mr Equinox, sent a text message concerning Katy's whereabouts to David Kingston, closing with, 'I think you had better get here, I will meet you in the Lagos office.'

A few days later the meeting took place. After the two men discussed the best plan of finding Katy, David Kingston made a phone call to a friend in Lagos, a wizard with computers. His instructions were to hack into the computer of the hotel where Katy was staying in Botswana and find an address. To this expert, that was no problem, and soon Jennifer's name and her office address was in Kingston's possession.

David Kingston hired a car and began the long journey to Lusaka, Zambia in search of Miss Katy Galloway. Meanwhile, Mr Equinox booked a flight to the UK.

Chapter 10 - Oluwaseyi

Kingston sat in his car a short distance from Jennifer's office. As he waited, Kingston thought back to the Isle of Man and his association with James Walters. Walters had set up the 'Isle of Man Property Company' and persuaded him to come on board as a director and young Joel Galloway as an associate. Walters, however, had received threats from business acquaintances he had defrauded. Wanting to leave no trace behind, and without telling his wife Jane, he had absconded to Lagos, Nigeria where he proceeded to set up a new company with African directors. The directors were Victor Oluwaseyi and Benjamin Adebayo. Victor was a shrewd businessman who very soon took command of the African projects.

One of the schemes was the sale of part of the Isle of Man northern plain to an American entrepreneur named Jacob Levinson. On a brief visit back to the Isle of Man, incognito of course, Walters had met with Levinson in the recently opened Northern Hotel. A competent conman, Walters had produced documentation proving that he owned a considerable portion of land in Ayre on the northern plain. David Kingston, who was present at the meeting and acting as an advocate, remembered how Levinson, after visiting the area, was convinced that this would be an ideal situation for a golf resort. The bogus advocate then produced a contract which stated that Jacob Levinson had agreed to purchase from the Isle of Man Property Company the area designated therein etc. etc. Jacob Levinson had requested the documents to show to his lawyer and they agreed to meet the following day at his hotel in Douglas. Walters, who did not want to be recognised in Douglas, apologised that other business prevented him from attending the meeting. Always the confident conman he suggested that he sign the documents there and then and leave the rest to his advocate and fellow director David Kingston. Jacob Levinson agreed, and the meeting duly took place during which, satisfied that all was in order, Jacob Levinson and David Kingston signed. Levinson said that business also meant a swift return to the States, but when he received a copy of the contract and sales notice he would forward to the Isle of Man Property Company account the agreed down payment of £5000.

A UK office was set up in Glasgow from which he and Walters operated. Joel Galloway became their 'goffer' but, had not deposited the documents pertaining to the sale in the company's bank. In a letter to Kingston Joel stated that because of loyalty to his family he had decided to resign. He no longer felt comfortable about the company dealings especially with regards to Mr Levinson whom he regarded as a nice gentleman. The letter went on to say that the offending documents were concealed in a safe place. Joel had died without revealing where he had hidden the documents.

Walters then assigned Kingston the task of recovering the documents as quickly as possible because Oluwaseyi was (rightly) convinced that he and Kingston were attempting to defraud him and Oluwaseyi was not a man to be crossed. He had underworld connections, and his last phone call to Walters contained threats of revenge and his resignation from the company effective as soon as he received his share of the monies owed.

Just then his reverie was broken by the arrival of Katy, who entered the office and a short time later emerged with an African lady whom Kingston assumed was Jennifer. He watched as Jennifer drove from the office car park and followed the car. It stopped, and Katy alighted outside a school. Kingston watched as she entered and then noted the name of the school. He was about to park and follow her in when his mobile rang.

It was James Walters also known as – Mr Equinox.

'Hi, where are you?' he asked.

'Sitting outside a school in Lusaka where I think Katy Galloway works. Why?' responded David Kingston.

Walters told him that he had just received word from a contact in Lagos that Adebayo was found dead in a police cell this morning. He had no other details but suggested that Kingston should forget Katy and get back to the UK office and wind things up there.

'I will text you my new address in Manchester,' said Walters, 'Contact me when you get back to the UK.'

'That's unwelcome news,' said Kingston frowning, 'But I still want to contact Miss Galloway before I leave. I'll keep a low profile.'

He ended the call before his caller could make any response. The text arrived with the relevant information, and David Kingston decided to have a coffee and browse the news about his fellow director.

Adebayo had resigned his position some time ago on health grounds, and the verdict was death by heart failure. He had, however, an association with another company from which he had embezzled funds.

'Good riddance,' Kingston said to himself, but inwardly he felt a surge of fear as he pondered the present whereabouts of Victor Oluwaseyi. He had, however, never met Victor Oluwaseyi in person but had spoken to him once on the phone so – why worry?

Chapter 11 – Move

When Katy had completed her first month, the mission furnished her with a car which meant she no longer needed to rely on Jennifer. She only used the car for travelling to schools and for the occasional visit to the shopping mall. On visits to headquarters, she travelled with Jennifer.

On one of Katy's teaching days, she stopped to ask Miss Ungoni, the school secretary, a question. Katy's mouth gaped open in horror at the face on the monitor of the outside door camera. It was the face of a man she thought she would never see again; David Kingston was asking the secretary if he could speak to Miss Galloway. Miss Ungoni turned to look at Katy only to see her shocked expression. Katy shook her head violently and ran down the corridor in tears and out the rear school door. She drove to the outskirts of town and parked her car. She phoned the school and when Miss Ungoni answered, Katy apologised and explained that David Kingston was a dangerous man. The school secretary informed Katy that when she saw her distress, she told the man that Miss Galloway was not in school at present and suggested he should call back later.

'I contacted Mr Kabaghe, and he took over your class,' explained Miss Ungoni, 'What do you plan to do? The Kingston character has gone.'

Katy thanked her and said she would return and explain the circumstances. She drove back to school and met with the principal, Mr Kabaghe. Katy apologised for having left school so abruptly and explained that David Kingston was a dangerous individual from the Isle of Man:

'I believe he was responsible for my brother's death and, on several occasions, had sent me threatening letters.'

'Miss Ungoni contacted me, and I called into your class and gave your assistant some test papers for the pupils to do and was about to ring Jennifer when you returned.'

Just then, the phone in the office rang.

'Mr Kabaghe,' Miss Ungoni said, 'That gentleman is at the door again – the one who frightened Miss Galloway.'

'Right,' said the principal, 'Let him in.'

He ended the call and then telephoned the police station and explained the situation.

'The police are sending officers,' Mr Kabaghe said to Katy, 'You wait here, and I will talk to the gentleman.'

With that, he left the office and proceeded to the reception area, stopping first at Miss Ungoni's office window.

'Show no surprise at anything I say,' he said to her, 'But while I am speaking to the gentleman, ring my mobile three times and stop.'

'Good morning, sir,' Mr Kabaghe greeted David Kingston and invited him into the foyer, 'How can I help you? I believe you were enquiring after Miss Galloway.'

'That's right' said Kingston, 'I had work to do in this area and I discovered she taught here. Her brother, who died recently, was a friend of mine and I thought I would pass on my condolences.'

'Miss Galloway only works here occasionally,' replied Mr Kabaghe, 'She comes in a few days a month to teach English.'

Just then his mobile rang, 'Excuse me.'

Mr Kabaghe spoke again to Kingston, 'That message was to say that she could no longer visit the school. Apparently, she fell ill a few days ago. It must have been serious because the hospital has flown her back to the UK.'

David Kingston sneered and was about to speak when he saw a police car enter the car park. He turned and abruptly left the school building, walking, as Mr Kabaghe observed, in the opposite direction from the incoming police.

Two policemen left their vehicle and walked towards the school entrance. Mr Kabaghe held the door open, invited them in and asked them to follow him to his office.

Once inside, he introduced them to Katy, and they reviewed the day's events. Mr Kabaghe said that his secretary would download the man's picture from her disc, and they could have it:

'If he is known to you, you can still apprehend him.'

There was a knock at the door, and Miss Ungoni appeared, carrying a tray containing cups of coffee.

When the policemen left, Mr Kabaghe turned to Katy and said, 'Now, young lady, go home, and I will call later this evening, and we we'll talk.'

Katy pulled her coat hood up and walked swiftly to her car. She was glad when she arrived at her lodgings.

Katy was troubled. If Kingston had somehow traced her to Zambia, he could cause trouble for Jennifer and perhaps the school. She remembered the threatening letters which she now knew had come from David

Kingston, and she was convinced that he had something to do with her brother Joel's death. She hated the thought of it but decided that for her and the school's sake, she would once again have to leave Zambia. Her love for Africa had grown steadily over the years and she desperately wanted to stay – but where? She just knew she had to leave Zambia.

Once again Katy searched the situations vacant columns, this time on her laptop. She looked at several schools in areas outside of Zambia and came across a school in Tanzania – the Kilimanjaro Girls Secondary School.

Katy googled it and was impressed by what she saw. The school was looking for a history teacher and the job description suited Katy admirably. She copied the details and waited for the visit of her school principal.

At seven o'clock that evening, Mr Kabaghe rang the doorbell of Katy's lodgings, and Mrs Buxton invited him in.

'Katy told me what happened at school,' she said, 'You can use my snug for your conversation.'

Mrs Buxton then called to Katy and informed her that her boss had arrived and was in the snug.

They settled into Mrs Buxton's snug with coffee.

Mr Kabaghe was about to speak when Katy stopped him.

'I have made a decision,' she said and showed Mr Kabaghe the Kilimanjaro school details on her laptop.

Her school principal laughed and produced a laptop from his briefcase. Opening it, he showed Katy the very same advertisement.

'I spent some time in prayer after you left today, and I am convinced that God had a hand in both of our decisions,' he said, 'The headmistress of the girl's school is my sister. Her name is Mrs Jeffers, and I knew of her need for a history teacher. This afternoon when I looked through your credentials I noticed that your master's degree was in history. I phoned her and emailed her your status. She phoned back to suggest that you go there for an interview as soon as possible. I suggested in two days, and she agreed. Although this isn't a mission school, and it is just for girls, I think that the Kilimanjaro Girls Secondary school would suit you, that is if you want to stay in Africa.'

'Oh yes,' said Katy, 'I want to complete my time in Africa; this man Kingston was stalking me in the Isle of Man and has obviously followed me out here. There is another man who approached me in Botswana; he called himself Mr Equinox and said he knew me from the Isle of Man. Perhaps he told Kingston where I was.'

'Right,' said Mr Kabaghe, 'So what do you want to do?'

'I will go for the interview,' replied Katy, 'But you need to promise me something: I don't want anyone else knowing where I am, not even Jennifer. I will leave a letter of resignation in her office tomorrow and leave for Tanzania. Will you please contact your sister and then tell me how and where to go?'

'I will do more than that,' replied Mr Kabaghe, 'I will take you there. It will be an excuse for a few days off and to see my sister. I will phone her tonight and tell her your decision. You pack your things tonight, and I will collect you tomorrow after I sort things with my deputy at school. I will also contact the other school principals and inform them that for personal reasons you can no longer visit their schools.'

'Thank you,' said Katy, 'I do appreciate what you are doing for me.'

Her principal then shook her hand and said, 'The school and I will miss you, but it is for the best, good night.'

Katy wrote a letter of resignation to Jennifer in which she explained about Kingston and that due to the recent circumstances, it would be better if Jennifer didn't know where she was.

The next morning, she phoned Jennifer and apologised that, for personal reasons, she couldn't come to the office that day. Jennifer asked no questions but hoped everything would be okay for the following day.

* * * *

The journey to Dar es Salaam was by plane—Fastjet via Harare—and took just under four hours. During the flight, Mr Kabaghe told her some of his family history. His sister was a widow whose husband, Frank Jeffers, an Englishman, worked with the Tanzanian government. He suffered a heart attack and died when he and his wife were on holiday in England; she buried him there in his hometown.

Two days later, Katy, who now introduced herself as Katherine, had her interview with the board of Kilimanjaro Girls Secondary School. The members, pleased with what they heard, asked her if she could start immediately. They explained that the school was residential and hoped she wouldn't mind living in. Katy said that would suit her very well.

That evening when she was unpacking, Katy discovered she had left a copy of the Aire documents in one of Jennifer's desk drawers along with her school reports and visitation rota. As far as she could remember there was nothing left with Jennifer that would lead anyone to find her.

The next morning, Katherine joined the rest of the staff for breakfast and was introduced. Later that day she took a bus into town and visited a mobile phone shop where she bought a new SIM card. The staff member installed it and set up a new mobile number on her phone. So, began Katherine's new life in Tanzania.

Chapter 12 - Discoveries

Simon watched from his hotel window as the moon, released from its cloudy prison, washed the night away from the Isle of Man's northern plain. The Old House, bathed in the moon's silvery glow, took on a ghostly appearance that filled him with a sense of foreboding. He recalled with sadness the tragedy that had occurred in the stables there. A tragedy that not only brought heartache to Katy and her family but had had serious ramifications. Funny, he thought, as nostalgia crept in, the house has a majestic name, yet we, as children, always called it *'The Old House'*.

Almost a year had passed since Katy had left for Africa leaving no news of her whereabouts. Various attempts had been made to contact her but all in vain. It was as though Africa had swallowed her up.

Simon turned away from the window and lay on his hotel bed. Seeing the Old House again brought back so many memories. He realised how much he missed the Isle of Man, his school and college friends and Katy. In his mind, he was once again standing with Katy and Joel on the platform in Ramsey waiting for the electric train to take them to the top of the island's highest point, Snaefell summit. He remembered from his history class that Snaefell, at over 2000 feet above sea level, was the island's only mountain. On a clear day they could see six kingdoms; the Isle of Man, England, Scotland, Wales, Ireland and Heaven. He recalled with fondness the three friends sitting in the mountaintop café enjoying strawberry milkshakes. He remembered the school trips to Port Erin; first on the electric train from Ramsey to Douglas, then along the promenade on the horse-drawn carriage to catch the steam train south. Simon fell asleep dreaming of times gone by and woke the next morning, his mind still full of memories.

He put the memories of the past aside and focused on the present and the purpose of his visit: to seek information about Katy. Not long after her trip to Donegal, she had disappeared off the radar. Simon had decided that the Isle of Man would be the best place to start his search, so during his vacation he travelled once again to his former homeland. He had tried to call Katy several times, both last night and this morning, but without success.

After breakfast, he walked from his hotel to Kingsway Mansion. The March air was a balm to his freshly shaved face, and he enjoyed the walk in the pale sunshine. As he approached the house, he noticed a black Lexus parked a few metres from the drive entrance. Simon continued up the drive. Despite the car's presence, the house looked deserted. He heard no sound when he pressed the doorbell, and there was no response to his knock on the door. Simon went around to the kitchen entrance and looked in through the windows. He could see no furniture inside, and he found the kitchen entrance door unlocked. Stepping inside, Simon noticed footprints on the dusty floor – certainly a man's. Simon moved on into the large hallway he knew so well, where he and Joel had played ball games upon which Lord Galloway had frowned.

He opened the first door to the snug often used by Lord Galloway and his various acquaintances. Then the next door, and the next. Each door opened to empty rooms, rooms that brought back so many memories. Suddenly, the ringing of a phone broke the eerie silence of the house. There was no sign of a house phone, so Simon followed the sound back to the snug. This time, he entered the room. Behind and previously hidden by the open door, he found the source of the ringing. It was coming from a man sprawled on the floor of the snug, his sightless eyes open towards the ceiling. The phone had stopped ringing, but Simon could now see it in the outstretched hand of the obviously dead body. A ray of sunlight entered through the window causing Simon to look in that direction. That is when he noticed another phone, on the windowsill and one he recognised. Keeping close to the wall to not intrude on the part of the room where the body lay, Simon made his way towards the window. The letter K on the phone cover confirmed what he suspected; it was Katy's phone. Simon retraced his footsteps and looked again at the dead man. He was staring at a crime scene, evident by the amount of blood which had poured from the gaping hole in the neck of the corpse. Taking out his mobile phone, Simon dialled 999.

※ ※ ※ ※

The island's pagan community celebrated the summer and winter solstices, but equinox passed with seldom a mention. An equinox, Simon recalled, is an astronomical event in which the plane of Earth's equator passes through the centre of the sun. It occurs twice each year, around 20th March and 23rd September. As Simon waited in the hall for the arrival of the police, his phone informed him that this day, the 20th March 2006, was the Spring Equinox.

At that moment, Simon wondered if his life was at an equinox, with the past measurable and the future uncharted. Would his future timeline just equal his past? Was it this sight of death that caused him to think like this? Faced with this sobering reminder of his mortality, Simon uttered a silent prayer of thanksgiving remembering that his time was in God's hands.

Nevertheless, he shuddered and was relieved to hear a knock at the front door. He opened the door to admit a plainclothes police officer, accompanied by a Constable in uniform. Simon explained that the house belonged to a family friend. He had been looking for her, found the kitchen door open and heard the mobile phone ringing. He explained that, since finding the body in the snug, he had touched nothing.

'Who and where is your friend?' asked the plainclothed officer.

'Her name is Katy Galloway, and this was her family home. I hoped she would be here,' said Simon, 'But she may still be in Africa; she's working with a missionary organisation there.'

The officer introduced himself as Inspector Johnson and said, 'I would like you to report to the police station and make a statement.'

Simon agreed, then added that the phone on the windowsill belonged to his friend, Katy. The inspector nodded but made no comment, so Simon left Kingsway Mansion. He began walking down the drive when he remembered the Lexus. Retracing his steps, he told the inspector about the black Lexus and explained that it wasn't his. The inspector thanked him and said he would have forensics search the deceased's pockets for car keys.

Simon nodded and again left to walk back to his hotel. On arrival, he went to his car and began the drive to Douglas to the police station. Inside the station, he explained to the desk Sergeant who he was and why he'd come. The desk Sergeant asked Simon to take a seat and disappeared down an adjoining corridor. A few minutes later, he returned with another officer, who introduced himself as Chief Constable Caley and invited Simon to follow him to his office.

'So,' began the Chief Constable, 'You found the body?'

'Yes,' replied Simon. He went on to explain why he had been at the house: 'I was brought up in that house. Its name is Kingsway Mansion and it belonged to Lord and Lady Galloway. My mother used to be the house-keeper for the family. I was in Scotland when another death occurred there; the son of the family hanged himself in the stables. His sister Kate received several threatening letters and rented out the house and moved to Douglas where she taught for some years in the grammar school. Katy then went to Africa on a short-term mission with the African Missionary Society. Later she applied and was accepted for a longer period of mission. She may still be in Africa, but I don't know where; we lost touch and I thought I might have found a clue in the house as to where she was. The house was open when I got there and then I found the dead man. I'm not sure why the house was empty and void of fur-niture, but I intend to make inquiries while I am here.'

The Chief Constable said that while he hadn't known Lord and Lady Galloway, he did know of Katy; she had taught one of his grandchildren. He buzzed an intercom and asked for a pad and pen that a Constable soon brought to his office.

'I'll leave you to it,' the Chief Constable said, 'I have another engagement to attend.' He then opened a drawer and produced a large brown envelope, which he handed to Simon: 'Sign your statement, put it in the envelope, and leave it on my desk.'

Then, with a wave of his hand, he donned his cap and left Simon to record the events of the morning.

* * * *

After leaving the police station, Simon drove back to his hotel and had lunch. He then phoned the school where Katy taught, only to be told that she had not worked there since September of last year and that the school had no forwarding address. Simon lay on his bed, pondering why Katy had left the island without getting in touch, why her phone was in Kingsway and who could shed some light on all of this. He decided that the first thing to do would be to discover who her friends were. He phoned the school again and asked the secretary if Katy had been friendly with any of the other teachers. She told him that Katy often had lunch with Miss Wilson, a former teacher who was now retired. Simon's plea for contact information finally charmed the secretary; she gave him the address of a Mrs March who lived in Onchan, and her telephone number. He thanked her and rang off.

He phoned the number, and after quite a few rings, a voice said, 'Hello? Who's calling?'

Simon replied, 'Am I speaking to Mrs March, a friend of Miss Wilson?'

'Oh yes, this is Emily March, and Miss Wilson is a friend who used to visit me. And who are you?' asked Mrs Emily March.

Simon quickly explained the situation.

'Oh, wee Simon, Jane's son,' crooned Mrs March, 'I remember you. I used to visit Lady Galloway at Kingsway Mansion, and I remember you, Katy and Joel playing there. So sad about Joel, and the house is now lying empty. What a shame.'

Mrs March then informed Simon that Katy had lodged with her for a while and that Miss Wilson, Eileen, often visited:

'We played Scrabble together,' she said. He could hear a smile in her voice: 'But I had no chance against school teachers.'

She then added that she missed Katy but had no idea of her present whereabouts, 'Miss Wilson might know, however; she now lives in Donegal.'

'Do you know where in Donegal?' asked Simon, 'Have you a contact number?'

'Of course,' came the reply, 'We still keep in touch. But how do I know you are who you say you are?'

Simon assured her he was the 'wee' Simon of Kingsway and gave her some details only he would know. Mrs March paused, and then, after some thought, gave Simon the Donegal number.

He quickly disconnected, then phoned the new number.

A polite voice answered, 'Hello. 482, Eileen Wilson speaking.'

'Hello, Miss Wilson,' said Simon, 'This is Simon Walters; I'm a friend of Katy Galloway.'

'Oh, yes,' Miss Wilson interrupted, 'She often spoke of you. How are you?'

'I'm fine, but I am worried about Katy. Have you heard from her recently?'

Eileen Wilson told him that Katy had visited her last October and said something about missionary work somewhere in Zambia with the African Missionary Society and had travelled there in November. She added that Katy had left a small box behind, which contained lots of paperwork. Miss Wilson explained that she had seen Katy looking through the papers on several occasions. She had no idea what they contained, but in her last letter, Katy had sent some photographs and asked her to put them in the box, along with the other things.

'You are welcome to come and look through them,' said Miss Wilson, 'I haven't heard from her in ages. Katy didn't include an address with the photographs she sent.'

Simon thanked Miss Wilson and gave her his mobile number before ending the call. His heart was telling him to go to Donegal and continue the investigation into Katy's sudden departure, but his head reminded him of his obligations. Next morning, he signed out of his hotel and caught the early ferry to Liverpool. Then he drove the long journey back to Edinburgh.

As Simon carried out his tasks of visiting and preaching, the weeks flew by so quickly that he had to put his plans to look for Katy on hold. He did, however, keep in touch with Miss Wilson, who informed him that she had still heard nothing of Katy. Simon explained to her that the extent of his church work meant postponing his visit to Donegal until late spring or early summer. A surprise awaited him, however, when, one evening, on returning home from work, Simon found a large parcel awaiting him, accompanied by a note. Miss Wilson had gathered all Katy's paperwork and files and parcelled them, along with some mementoes, for him to look over in his spare time. Later that evening, Simon telephoned and thanked Miss Wilson for her thoughtfulness.

After supper, Simon and his mother set about sorting out the parcel of paraphernalia belonging to Katy. Most were personal items, including her journal which he gave to his mother to look through.

'Simon,' Jane said, 'The back of her journal contains some of her contact numbers and addresses, but not ours. Perhaps she couldn't get in touch with us because her main contacts are probably on her mobile phone.'

As Simon searched through the rest of the journal, he soon discovered that Katy was frightened, but of whom, she didn't say. Other papers related to the African Mission Society. Other leaflets involved teaching English as a foreign language. As he turned one of them over, he read, in Katy's handwriting:

Why did Joel not go to Africa? What made him change his mind and stay? Why do I feel that David Kingston has something to do with Joel's death? Katy had written down these questions but had provided no answers.

He then found Joel's note to Katy.

The addition regarding him and Katy made Simon smile. The thought had, at one time, crossed his mind. Simon read the letter again and then remembered that David Kingston was the shady character the Chief Constable had warned Lord Galloway about; Simon wondered if he was still on the Isle of Man. He and his mother gathered everything together and his mum stored them in her writing bureau.

* * *

That night, Simon had a dream. He was making his way through a jungle, cutting aside swathes of grass and brush with a large machete. Suddenly, he emerged into a clearing with a grass hut. Gingerly, he approached and noticed the grass door pulled aside. Simon looked in and there, sleeping on a camp bed, was Katy. He approached her and softly touched her on the shoulder, speaking her name. Then he recoiled in horror as the figure on the bed arose. It wasn't Katy; it was an African witch doctor, and across his hat was written the word: *EQUINOX*.

Simon woke with a start, sweat pouring from his forehead. The sun was shining through his bedroom window and lighting up a framed text on the wall. The lovely, challenging and reassuring words were from Scripture: 'Trust in the Lord with all your heart and lean not on your own understanding.' The words were from Proverbs 3:5. Simon picked up his towel, knelt by his bed and sought the Lord for guidance and wisdom. After his shower, he met his mum for breakfast and shared his dream with her.

'Well,' said his mother, with a smile on her face, 'You know the Bible also says that your young men will dream dreams.'

At that, they both smiled and tucked into breakfast.

Afterwards, Jane said she would find out what she could about the African Mission Society, to see if they could shed any light on Katy's whereabouts. Simon said he would continue the investigation and catch up with her at dinnertime.

It was all Simon could do to concentrate on his work that morning; he was glad of the opportunity to do some pastoral visits that helped the afternoon to race by. Back in the office, Alice, one of the volunteer staff, told him that his mum had phoned and wanted him to get in touch ASAP.

Simon thanked her and pounded the numbers on his phone.

His mother answered on the first ring, 'Oh Simon,' she exclaimed, 'I wanted to talk to you sooner, but I didn't want to use your mobile. Hurry home – we have lots to talk about.'

With that, she ended the call before Simon could say a word.

The last period at work seemed to drag, but at last, with his office tasks in order, Simon made his way home. Of all evenings, the traffic through Edinburgh was terribly slow, much to Simon's frustration. But, at last, he drew into the allotted parking space outside his mum's apartment. Breathless, he climbed the stairs – ignoring the lift – and opened the apartment door. His mum was waiting for him, sitting at the kitchen table, with various pages spread out before her.

'Right,' said Simon. 'Tell me what has you so excited.'

'This,' Jane replied, showing him several of Katy's photos.

Pointing to one, she told Simon that the man in the photograph was his father. Simon stared at the picture and wondered why Katy would have taken it. Jane then showed him the back of the photo. There was a date: August 2006.

'So, this is my father,' said Simon, 'and he is—or was—in Africa.'

Looking again at the photo, he thought that his father had probably not been aware of being photographed unless he'd seen the camera later.

'I wonder if Katy was the photographer,' Simon said, thinking aloud, 'I remember her using her phone to take pictures at my graduation. They weren't great. What if someone else took the photos and sent them to her? Was there an envelope with them?'

'Yes, of course,' said his mum, tut-tutting at herself for overlooking something so obvious. She reached into the box and brought out an envelope, 'I think you are right, Simon. Look at the postmark.'

The postmark on the envelope said *Zambia*.

'Mum, do you still have the Sheffield number of the African Missionary Society?'

Jane looked it up on her phone and handed it to Simon. He googled the African Missionary Society and dialled the displayed phone number.

A lady answered: 'Hello. The African Mission Society, Marjory Downs speaking. How can I help you?'

'I am trying to contact one of your former missionaries, Katy Galloway,' replied Simon.

'Oh,' said Marjory in a surprised voice, 'Katy is popular. That's the third request we have had for her in the last few weeks.'

'I know,' Simon interrupted, 'My mother phoned recently. But you said there were three calls?'

'Yes,' came the reply, 'Katy's brother, Joel, phoned only yesterday from the Isle of Man. I tried to call him back, but his phone was no longer in use. I thought that rather strange.'

'He did say it was her brother, Joel?' Simon asked.

'Oh, yes,' Marjory responded, 'He said he was phoning from his and Katy's home on the Isle of Man. Sure enough, when I checked, it was Katy's home phone number. But, as I said, when I tried to return the call, I was informed that the number was no longer in use.'

'Could you connect me with someone in Zambia who knows Katy?'

Marjory gave him the phone number and address of one of the mission's local directors, Jennifer Holmes. She and Katy had been in contact several times.

'What is it?' asked his mum, after he'd disconnected, 'You've gone pale.'

He recounted his conversation with the lady at the mission centre. For a while, Simon his mum both stared at each other, speechless.

Simon broke the silence. 'Would you phone Jennifer and make some inquiries? I need to go and talk to my senior pastor, Graham, because you and I have to go to Zambia.'

Jane made the phone call and spoke to Jennifer. She learned that Jennifer had lost contact with Katy. However, the women exchanged mobile numbers and arranged to meet once Jane and Simon arrived in Zambia.

* * * *

Simon told Graham about Katy's African connection and explained that he hadn't heard from her since she went there with the African Missionary Society. He then asked if the Church leadership would grant him time off to pay a short visit to Africa.

Graham met with the leadership the next day and outlined Simon's situation regarding Katy and Africa. He reminded them that, as part of their missionary out-reach, the Craiglockhart Church supported a young African Christian fellowship, both prayerfully and financially. He suggested that the church leadership send Simon to the fellowship with a gift and a message of encouragement. Afterwards, he could stay on and enquire after Katy. His leadership colleagues agreed, and Graham reported back to a delighted Simon.

He called around to his mum's apartment and shared the good news that evening, and she relayed to him what Jenifer had told her on the phone.

'Katy spent a short time in Zambia and, on returning home, was accepted by the mission for longer service. She taught for a while when she was in Zambia, but then, for some reason, she disappeared. Jennifer said she would provide more information when we arrive.'

By the end of the week, Jane and Simon had packed and, with Simon's financial arrangements sorted, were on their way. Simon was pleased to have his mother, who paid her personal expenses, go with him; he appreciated her godly wisdom. He left his car in Jane's apartment car park and they took a taxi to Edinburgh airport.

Chapter 13 - Africa

The fellowship Simon had to visit was in Malawi, and although the journey there was uneventful, his time with the fellowship was both interesting and exciting. He and Jane were met at Zomba Airport by the pastor, Reverend Alfred Mumba, and driven to his home, where they met his wife, Melina. Over dinner, Alfred told them that he had studied at Glasgow University and met Graham there. Graham had also been a student, and, as Christians, they had attended church together. When Alfred returned to Malawi, he studied theology at the Zomba Theological College. Afterwards, he and a few Christian friends founded the Zomba Christian Fellowship. He and Graham had corresponded regularly; the Zomba Fellowship appreciated the support of their Scottish brothers and sisters.

Simon presented Alfred with the Craiglockhart Church gift, and for the next few days, he and Jane stayed with Alfred and Melina. On Sunday, Simon and Jane met with the church fellowship, and Simon shared a message from his home church. Pastor Alfred preached a challenging sermon on Proverbs 3: 5–6, reminding Simon of his dream about the witch doctor and Equinox. That evening, Alfred told them that flying would be the best way to travel to Zambia and offered to pay for their flights. Jane thanked him, but graciously declined the offer, assuring him she had sufficient funds to cover their journey.

Simon had made a study of Zambia on his iPad in the days before his departure, so he knew quite a bit about its history and culture. Although he knew that the usual greeting was *Muli Bwanji*, expressed with cupped hands, he also learned that many now greeted English speakers with a *hello* and a handshake. His mother, however, was a little concerned to learn that women were usually silent in the presence of men and that they kept their distance. Neither of them needn't have worried, however.

Early on Monday morning, as previously arranged, they were met at the airport by Jennifer and a Zambian gentleman, whom she introduced as Alinani. As he shook Simon warmly by the hand and embraced Jane, kissing her on both cheeks, he said, with a wide smile, that most folk just called him Alan. Alan drove. Simon sat beside him, while Jane and Jennifer chatted in the back. As he drove, Alinani explained that he was a district director of the African Missionary Society and was responsible for overseeing the work in Zambia and Tanzania. The mission was divided into thirty districts throughout Zambia and Tanzania, and each district had a director; Jennifer was his assistant director, and they were based in Lusaka.

Soon, they were driving through the streets of Lusaka to the Mission Station. As yet, no one had mentioned Katy; it was not until Simon and Jane were seated in the director's air-conditioned office that Jennifer brought up the subject.

'Since you told me you were coming, Jane,' said Jennifer, 'I went to our headquarters in Dodoma, where

I had mentioned your enquiry to Alan; we looked through Katy's files but there was nothing there to help us discover where she might have gone. We thought she might have gone back to the Isle of Man, but the UK office couldn't help.'

Jennifer then told her guests that she had phoned Katy's landlady, Mrs Buxton, who told her that Katy and Mr Kabaghe, the school principal, had gone to visit his sister. Katy had all her belongings with her and had settled her account, but Mrs Buxton had no idea where Mr Kabaghe's sister lived.

'All applications are kept at headquarters,' Jennifer said, 'But her activities were stored here. Katy was well liked. She was a good teacher, and I enjoyed her company. I wonder if Mr Equinox had anything to do with her sudden departure?'

'Mr Equinox?' asked Simon.

Jennifer then explained about Mr Equinox and the holiday she and Katy had taken during Katy's first visit to Zambia.

'Do you know anything about these?' asked Jane, taking an envelope from her shoulder bag and opening it to display the photographs from Katy's box, the one left with Miss Wilson.

She showed them to Jennifer, who smiled and said, 'Oh, yes! Katy and I took these while we were on holiday in Botswana. It was when Katy came out here to see if this is, as she put it, where God wanted her to be. We both hit it off right away, and as I had some leave due, off we went to Botswana.'

Picking out the photo that showed her husband, Jane asked, pointing to the man in the picture, 'Do you recognise this man?'

'Yes,' replied Jennifer, 'That is Mr Equinox.'

Alan looked at the picture, 'Oh, yes,' he said, 'I've met him. He came to headquarters some weeks ago, asking about Katy. Anyway, when I said I couldn't give out any personal details, he became quite irate and told me I was a . . . stuffed shirt. What is a *stuffed shirt?*'

Simon smiled, 'I believe he was saying you were full of your own self-importance,' he explained, 'Unfortunately, it isn't a compliment.'

'Oh.' Alan smiled in return, 'I'm only glad he didn't become violent; I would have had to show him what this *stuffed shirt* could do.'

They all laughed, but then sobriety returned to the conversation. Jennifer opened a drawer in her desk and withdrew a folder but held on to it as she continued:

'Well, would this help?' Jennifer asked, producing an important-looking document from the folder in her hand which she passed to Simon.

'Katy has the original, but she left this copy in her folder. Everything else in the folder pertains to her work here and is confidential.'

Jane and Simon gasped. They were looking at a copy of an Isle of Man Property Company sales notice and contract, which stated that, in September 1987, a Mr Jacob Levinson of New York had purchased the area known as *The Plain of Ayre*, on the Isle of Man, from IOM Property Company for five million dollars. It was signed Jacob Livingston. The other signatures at the bottom, titled as company directors, were James Walters and David Kingston. At the bottom of the contract the company and directors' names appeared again accompanied by another name – *Joel Galloway Associate Director*. At that, Jane collapsed into a chair burst into tears.

Through her sobs, she muttered, 'He was responsible, he was responsible.' Then, looking at the others, she went on, 'Don't you see? He was probably the reason that Joel committed suicide!'

Simon knelt and comforted his mother.

'She is talking about my father,' he explained, 'Who disappeared when I was a child. I don't remember him.'

'How could you?' Jane interrupted, 'You were just a baby.'

Simon went on to give Jennifer and Alan a brief summary of his childhood and his relationship with the Galloways. He ended with the mention that, one Saturday morning, Katy found Joel hanging in the stables, 'He was in his early twenties and working in an Isle of Man's government department. How he and my father met up, I can't imagine,'

Simon went on, 'I suppose it was possible that my father was still on the island, living under an assumed name. Oh! This is just too mind blowing.'

'How could he have been living on such a small island without meeting someone he knew from the past?' asked Jane, 'Unless, somehow, he was disguised or living in some remote area.'

'But what is his connection with Katy?' asked Jennifer. 'Surely, he would not have known her or met her.'

'Ah!' Alan remarked, joining in the conversation, 'What if it is the other way around? She might not have known him, but he would know of her and Joel, and, indeed, you, Simon, if he were living on the island.'

'I suppose he could have left and come back,' said Jane.

'I wonder,' said Alan, 'Would he, after leaving the Isle of Man, have come to Africa? I have friends in high

places who might help me discover if a James Walters—
or, perhaps, a Mr Equinox—was a resident in this part
of Africa in the 1990s or earlier. I'll leave you three pondering, while I go and make some telephone calls from
headquarters. Lovely to have met you, Jane and Simon.'

He shook their hands and promised to get in touch
as soon as he had any news.

After Alan departed, Jennifer made tea, and the threesome sat around the office table to discuss their next
move. Jennifer told Simon he could keep the documents
and give them to Katy if they should ever meet up.

Chapter 14 – Reunion

In the local Zambian office of the Africa Mission Society, Jennifer, Jane and Simon sat hunched over the desk, trying to make sense of their discoveries.

Jennifer looked at the photograph again.

'I remember taking this,' she said.' It was at a market in Francistown, in Botswana.' She smiled as the memories returned.

'Katy was—'

Just then, the office phone rang.

Jennifer answered with, 'Good afternoon, Africa Mission Society, Church Street office.'

'Hello Jennifer,' the caller said.

'Katy? Katy? What a coincidence; we were just talking about you. And, by the way, the 'we' includes Simon Walters and his mother, Jane.'

Some might say coincidence, but Simon knew it was the work of God. Jennifer handed the phone to Simon.

'Hello, Katy,' said Simon.

'What are you doing in Zambia?' she asked credulously.

'We are here looking for you,' he replied, 'We need to talk. So much has happened since we last met, and you are not answering our calls. Where are you?'

'Sorry about that; I'll explain when I see you. I'm in Tanzania; I teach in a girls' school. I was suddenly riddled with guilt because I had not been in touch with Jennifer.'

'You and I need to talk,' said Simon, 'My mum and I will make Tanzania our next port of call. Where in Tanzania are you?'

Katy then told Simon to send his mobile number to this phone and she would text details of her whereabouts and advise Simon and Jane how to get there but asked to speak again to Jennifer.

At that, Simon gave Jennifer the phone, so the women could continue their interrupted conversation. When they had finished talking, Simon sent his mobile number to Katy's phone. He then decided to travel to Tanzania.

'I think I'll apply for a job as a travel agent when I get home,' said Jane smiling.

'I cannot come with you; I'm needed here,' said Jennifer, 'But I will keep you up to date about Alan's findings.'

* * * *

The only last-minute flight from Lusaka to Dar es Salem, which Simon and Jane decided to book, left at 11.40 p.m. Simon phoned ahead and booked a twin-bedded room at a motel near the airport. The flight was uneventful and on time, so at a quarter to five in the morning, Simon and Jane were in their motel room, hoping to catch a few hours' sleep before breakfast. Simon had phoned earlier and told Katy their plans.

As he and Jane were settling their bill, the front door of the motel opened, and in walked Katy.

'Oh, how lovely to see you both,' she said, with a smile that seemed to light up her face.

Once they exchanged hugs, Katy ushered them outside to a waiting car and introduced a young man, the driver, as Joseph.

When Jane looked at her enquiringly, Katy just opened the rear door and ushered Jane in.

'It's a long story,' laughed Katy as they climbed into the car. 'I'd like Simon to hear it, so it will keep until later.'

Simon sat in the passenger seat beside Joseph. At times, he closed his eyes, as Joseph weaved alarmingly in and out of the morning traffic. Katy and Jane chatted in the back, seemingly unaware of the near-death experiences Simon was enduring. There was no conversation between Simon and Joseph; the latter was too busy concentrating on his driving, and the former unwilling to break that concentration.

On arriving safely at Katy's apartment, much to Simon's relief, he, Jane and Katy alighted. Joseph informed Simon, as he helped unload the luggage, that he was working to earn money to one day go to England and the Isle of Man. Simon wished him well as, with a wave and a beaming smile, Joseph drove off.

Katy explained about having met Joseph on the school away trip and, by coincidence, having come across him again when buying fish at the fish market. He was there with his grandmother, a lovely Swahili lady named Mila, with whom Katy had formed a friendship.

Later, drinking tea and eating scones that, Katy informed them, came from the local bakery, Katy shared what she knew of Joseph's background.

Mama Mila lived in a village on the outskirts of Dar es Salaam, the former capital city of Tanzania. All her life, she had lived near the sea, eaten from the sea, and travelled by sea. At eighty years of age, she was still able to start her boat's motor and catch enough fish to feed herself and take it to the nearby market. Her late husband, Joseph, had fished all his life and taught Mama Mila everything she knew about fishing and boating.

Her stamina, however, was not what it used to be; she tired quite easily. Mama Mila and Joseph had a daughter and two sons.

Adjah was the daughter's name, which meant *born on a Monday*. The boys were Joseph, named after his father, and Atieno, from Mama Mila's Swahili ancestors. Mila had seven grandchildren. One of them, the son of Joseph and also named Joseph, lived with her.

Joseph's great desire was to one day live and work in England. He currently attended college in Dar es Salaam, where he was studying English and History, but he loved, at weekends, going fishing with his gran. At college, he was an enthusiastic student, with A grades in all his exams. Joseph also loved Geology; he even attended after-school Geology classes. During the Autumn and Spring terms, his Geology class would visit the Mikumi National Park; this weekend trip, which included an overnight stay, was partly funded by the Education Authority. On one occasion, they had shared their tour with a group of girls from a girl's secondary school. During this tour, Joseph heard his teacher greet one of the girls' teachers as Miss Galloway. Her English accent had a lovely lilt. Joseph asked his teacher to introduce him to her, which he did. During their brief conversation, Joseph told her that, one day, he hoped to go to England. She told him that she came not from England, but from a British island called the Isle of Man and said that if he ever managed to get to England, he should look it up and pay it a visit. As Joseph turned away, she called to him, 'Give your teacher your address; I'll get it from him. When I return to the Isle of Man, I will write—I promise—and send you some information.'

When Joseph asked his teacher how he knew Miss Galloway, he was told that he had met her on another college outing.

Trip over, both groups stayed overnight at a local hostel before travelling back to Dar es Salem.

'Mila and Joseph take me out in their boat when I have a free weekend. She is a lovely lady.'

Katy also explained that Joseph's father had given him a second-hand car for his birthday and for graduating with honours from college.

'I taught him to drive, and as you noticed today, he is still learning. But, as my car is at present in the garage for repair, Joseph offered to drive me to the airport.'

Chapter 15 – Recollections

'Where do I begin?' said Katy. 'As you know from my letters, when I was in Africa on my first trip I learned from my agent that my tenants were moving out, so I asked him to close up the house until my return.'

She related that, on her return, she had cancelled her PO box and continued living in her home for a while, but she couldn't settle; Africa was in her blood and she wanted to return and continue her work there. So, she decided to sell. Katy planned to auction all the furniture and her dad's relics; she had already emptied the wardrobes and given all her family's clothes to charity.

'It was then, at home, that I found another letter; the tenants hadn't given it to my agent. Once again, it was from the anonymous writer. It stated that I had one week to deliver the material to the sender. It went on to say that Joel definitely had it and it was imperative that I find it. Then it said that, if I value my life, I must not open it, read the contents or involve the police. The writer this time gave me a PO box number in Douglas in the name of the IOM Property Company and a key. The letter prompted me to move to Douglas and I deposited the key in the PO box.'

She abruptly stood, 'Now, I need another cup of tea.'

After the welcome cuppa, Katy continued her story:

'I had already searched Joel's bedroom drawers and found nothing there. Dad had cleared most of his stuff and burned it. But then I remembered that Joel and I, as children, had a secret place where we would hide and play games and store our forbidden sweets and other things. It was in the part of the stables where Dad's stable man stored the feed for the horses. I found the envelope there. It contained a sales contract and a note from Joel.'

'I don't remember horses,' interrupted Simon.

'Of course, you don't,' said Katy, 'Mum told me that Dad had sold his horses to a friend who was starting up an equestrian centre somewhere in England. Apparently, whatever businesses my father was involved in took up more and more of his time, so the horses went there, and as far as I know, his stableman went there, too.'

'I did read the contents of the envelope; the note from Joel puzzled me because he was never in Africa. I recognised the name David Kingston, of course; he was the character the Chief Constable had mentioned to Dad. But the first name bothered me. I knew your surname was Walters, and I did know another family of that name who lived on the island, but, Jane, you had never mentioned your husband's first name to us as we were growing up.'

'I had put my husband out of my mind by the time I came to work again for your parents,' Jane explained.

Simon then told Katy about his visit to her house and finding a man's body there.

Simon suddenly remembered, 'The inquest is on Thursday next in Douglas, and I am a witness.'

'You never told me!' exclaimed Jane.

'No,' replied Simon, 'All the business of Katy put it out of my mind. You and I will need to go home for that.'

'Yes, well, to continue,' Katy interrupted, 'I had arranged for the auction company to clear all the furniture from the house, sell what they could, and give the rest to charity. The last letter that I received was more threatening. I remember the exact words: *I know you are home again. Your week is up, and I have decided you are not cooperating. You've got until tomorrow.'*

'That afternoon, the auctioneer arrived with his helpers and cleared the house. I gave Mrs March's address to the auctioneer, with instructions to give the address to no one and to send whatever monies were due me to Mrs March. Then I drove to Onchan. Mrs March made me welcome. Miss Wilson, my school colleague, also lodged with Mrs March. She had sold her house in Douglas and was planning to return home to Donegal, Ireland. I enjoyed my time with Mrs March, and I received no more threats, so I hoped I had given my threatening letter-writer the slip. Miss Wilson retired at the end of the school term and left the island to return to her Ireland home. She invited me to come and visit once she had settled in.'

'It was Mrs March who gave me her address,' Simon said, 'The school secretary knew you were staying with her.'

'That's right,' Katy explained. 'The school needed a forwarding address.'

'So, what happened to make you disappear from there?' asked Jane, 'Simon told me that even Mrs March didn't know where you had gone.'

'I felt awful about not confiding in her, but I didn't want to put her in danger,' Katy said.

'Why would Mrs March be in danger?' Simon enquired, 'Did something happen to make that possible?'

Katy told them about the shopping trip with Mrs March to the Tynwald Centre in St. Johns when a man had called out her name and said she was a difficult person to find. Katy explained how she knew right away that this was the letter-writer, and her suspicions were confirmed when he added that he'd expected a phone call from her. She also she realized that she had seen this man with Joel in Douglas; it was David Kingston, the man she suspected of murdering Joel.

Katy continued her story. 'I don't know what came over me, but I suddenly started to scream and call the police. The man left in a hurry and disappeared into the gathering crowd. The manager of the shopping centre arrived and led me to his office. Mrs March must have seen what had happened because she came alongside me and gave the manager our names. I apologised and asked him not to call the police, I said it was a misunderstanding.'

Katy explained that when they left the Tynwald Centre and were back at Mrs March's house, she explained the threatening letters and told Mrs March that she thought the man from the store was the letter-writer. That evening, she telephoned Miss Wilson and asked if she could stay with her in Donegal for a while. Miss Wilson asked no questions but said she would love to have company.

'So,' continued Katy, 'That same night, I packed my belongings, thanked Mrs March again for her hospitality and drove to Kingsway.'

Katy went on to say that when she unlocked the house she found two envelopes lying in the hallway. Katy recognised the writing and without opening them, put the letters into her bag to read later. After checking over the house and thankfully finding no major damage, she unpacked and read the letters. Like the others, they contained threats to herself, family and friends. Suddenly, she felt very frightened but collapsed on her bed and fell into an exhausted sleep. The next morning, she called the auction rooms and asked them to collect everything that was left. That same afternoon the auctioneer and helpers arrived, and Katy watched as the last of her family's belongings were loaded into the van. She then prepared for Donegal and Africa.

'As you two already know,' continued Katy, 'I had left a box of bits and pieces with Miss Wilson. But the notice about the sale of Ayre I took with me. Unfortunately, I foolishly left my mobile phone in Kingsway and didn't discover my loss until I tried to phone Miss Wilson. I bought another one in Dublin, but I only had a few numbers in my diary; yours weren't amongst them. All my main contacts were in my phone. That reminds me: I'd better give you my new number.'

'Oh!' she exclaimed delightedly, 'I also sold my car in Ireland for a decent price; with its low mileage, it went in a day. The rest of my journey was by bus and plane. Well, two planes, actually: one to Manchester and the other to Zambia. End of story; now, I need another cup of tea.'

Simon opened his travelling case and produced the sales copy.

'Here, you had better have this,' he said.

'Oh,' responded Katy, 'I'd forgotten about the copy. Why don't you hold on to it? Just in case anything happens to the original.'

Simon was about to protest when Katy looked at him with a puppy-dog expression and said, 'Please.'

Shaking his head and smiling, Simon returned the copy to his case.

Tea consumed, and phone numbers sorted, Jane asked, 'How did you end up in Tanzania?'

'David Kingston somehow discovered I worked in the school. I saw him and ran out in a panic. Later I went back to see the school principal and, to cut a long story short, he made me a proposition.'

'Not a proposal?' asked Jane, smiling.

'No!' retorted a shocked Katy, 'Just a proposition. I should have contacted Jennifer sooner to explain,' said Katy, 'But I was frightened that Kingston would have found out who she was and caused her harm.'

Katy then talked briefly about how she came to be in Tanzania, her school and her new life.

'So, now we are up to date,' said Simon.

'And so, it's back to the UK and Isle of Man for us. And what about you?' asked Jane.

'Well,' replied Katy, 'I would love to accompany you, now that school summer holidays have begun'

Just then the phone rang. It was Jennifer to say that Alan had made enquiries and discovered that James Walters and David Kingston were in partnership with two Lagos gentlemen whose names he didn't know but they were in the property business. Walters and Kingston had made several trips to Lagos over the past five years and were known in Lagos hotels. That is all his contacts could discover. Katy thanked him and told Jennifer of her plans spend her summer holidays in the UK.

That evening Simon booked their flights to London and Edinburgh.

Chapter 16 – The Isle of Man

Their journey was almost at an end. The plane descended from the sunshine, through the clouds, to a British summer and rain. Of course, British summer weather wasn't always dominated by precipitation; London had plenty of sunshine during the school holidays. Today, though, Jane, Simon and, especially, Katy welcomed the rain, after what had been an arid and hot time in both Zambia and Tanzania.

As they made their way to the luggage reclamation centre, Katy asked, 'Simon, how long do you think you will spend on the Isle of Man?'

'Only until after the inquest. I have outstayed my time away from Craiglockhart,' he replied, 'Why do you ask?'

'Unbelievably, I feel homesick, especially for my house and homeland.' She sighed.

Simon responded, 'I don't like to think of you on your own there. Stay in Edinburgh with Mum. I'll prevail on my bosses for more time off; I'm sure they'll agree. Then you, Mum and I can fly to the Isle of Man.'

'Oh Simon, you are a star!' exclaimed Katy, throwing her arms around him.

The transfer to the Edinburgh plane went without a hitch. In just over two hours, the three weary travellers had landed, collected their luggage, hired a taxi and sat themselves down in Jane's apartment.

After an early supper, Jane organised the second bedroom for Katy. Simon said good night and drove to his apartment.

The next morning, Simon met Graham at a nearby café. After greeting each other warmly, Simon launched into the story of his African adventures. Graham decided that Africa had been a working endeavour, so Simon should take some vacation time.

Later that evening, Simon phoned his mum to say that he had booked a mid-morning flight for three from Glasgow to the Isle of Man. He also booked rooms at the Northern Hotel, where he had previously stayed.

Simon drove his car to Jane's apartment and left it there. The three then travelled by taxi to the bus station and boarded the Edinburgh to Glasgow bus. As the bus, with their luggage on board, made its way through the city traffic, Simon thought over his last visit to the Isle of Man. He looked forward to renewing his acquaintance with the Chief Constable and thought about the questions he wanted to ask. He also wanted to hear what, if any, were the results of the investigation into the death of the man whose body he had discovered.

∗ ∗ ∗ ∗

Their journey was uneventful and soon they were installed in the Northern Hotel on the Isle of Man.

'Did you know that this area was called the Plain of Ayre?' Simon asked Katy, as they sat drinking coffee in the hotel lounge.

'I remember learning about the northern plain from local geography, but I never heard it called the Plain of

Ayre,' she replied, 'I suppose the three conspirators invented this title, thinking it had more selling appeal. Oh, I hate to think of Joel as a conspirator.' Tears filled her eyes and rolled down her cheeks as Katy remembered her younger brother, 'I loved him so much.'

Simon knelt beside Katy's chair. He gave her his handkerchief and pulled her head down on his shoulder.

'My husband and this David fellow are the true villains,' Jane fumed, 'I wonder: are they still in Africa?'

'I have a feeling they will somehow follow the trail back here,' remarked Simon, 'After all, this island is where it all started.'

The next morning, after breakfast, Simon and Katy walked from the hotel to Kingsway Mansion. To Simon, even in the morning sunlight, the house took on menacing proportions. No longer did he consider it a formerly happy home, but a place now filled with memories of a sinister kind.

Katy broke into his reverie, 'I don't understand how they got in, neither the man who was murdered nor his killer!' Her voice was almost hysterical. Fumbling in her purse, she produced a set of keys.

'These, I thought, were the only keys to my home. I left all the other keys and some of my private items with my bank for safe keeping.'

'When I got here, the back door to the kitchen was unlocked. That's how I got in,' Simon responded, 'Did you use a safety deposit box?' he asked.

'Yes,' replied Katy. She showed Simon a key: 'This one and the one held by the bank are the only two keys.'

As Katy unlocked the front door, a police car entered the drive and stopped at the front of the house. Chief Constable Caley got out and approached them.

'I was informed that you were back on the island, Miss Galloway,' he said, 'And that you and your friends had checked into the Northern. I had my driver take me there, and I met your mother, Simon, having coffee in the lounge; she is looking well. It was she who told me where to find you both.'

Addressing Katy, he asked, 'Can we go inside, please? I need to ask you a few questions.'

Once inside, Katy led Simon and the Chief Constable into the hall.

'I'm sorry I can't offer you anything to drink, sir,' she said with a wry smile.

'I understand,' he responded, 'And, please, drop the sir. My name is Raymond. If you call me *sir*, I'll think you are one of my subordinates.' He smiled, 'Now, let's talk. You are aware, I'm sure, of what happened here. I need to know what, if anything, you can tell me.'

'I sold everything two years ago, locked up the house and left the island. I went to Donegal where I stayed for a time with a friend before leaving to work in Africa. I've not been back since . . . well, not until today.'

'We also have questions,' said Simon, 'Firstly –'

The Chief Constable held up his hand, 'Can I suggest that we retire to the comfort of your hotel, where I will buy the coffee? I will tell you what I know, and you can tell me what you know.'

Nothing more was said as they were driven to the hotel. On arrival, the Chief Constable dismissed his driver, saying that he would find his own way back to the station. As the threesome sat in the hotel lounge, waiting for their coffee, they were joined by Jane.

The Chief Constable rose to greet her, 'Hello again,' he said. Calling to the waiter, he asked for another coffee.

'How do you two know each other?' Simon asked.

'I was a member of the Isle of Man constabulary many years ago and was part of the team investigating your father's disappearance,' replied Raymond, 'That, I'm afraid, is still a mystery.'

'Not anymore,' Jane informed him, 'He turned up in Africa, but it's a long story.'

'It is, indeed,' said Simon, 'And you'll find he is part of your ongoing investigations.'

'Enlighten me,' urged Raymond.

'No, Chief Constable,' Simon countered, 'You need to bring us up to date on your investigation, please.'

The Chief Constable told them that the dead man discovered in Katy's home was a private detective named William Elliot. He had worked for a firm of insurance investigators in Manchester, but when contacted, they said they knew nothing of his visit to the Isle of Man, although they believed he may have been moonlighting for someone else. When the company checked his desk diary, they discovered the name Jacob in it for the day he died.

Raymond searched in his notebook, 'He wrote that day: *Mr Jacob Levinson re the plain – see Miss Galloway.* Does that mean anything to you?' he asked.

'It certainly does,' replied Katy. She searched through her shoulder bag, produced the bill of sale notice and handed it to Raymond.

'The Plain of Ayre?' he queried, 'I know of the Point of Ayre, but the Plain?'

'You're almost sitting on it,' smiled Katy, 'The land beyond this hotel is the Northern Plain, or as described in the document, The Plain of Ayre. Sounds more dramatic and alluring than *the Northern Plain*, don't you think?'

'How on earth's face did they con Mr Levinson, and who is he, anyway?' asked Raymond.

'Ah!' exclaimed Simon, 'I can help you there. Before I left my room this morning, I googled Mr Jacob Levinson. He is an American billionaire and property tycoon. He has villas in the Mediterranean and Spain, and that's just for starters. He has property all over Europe and America. And he owns the Cumberland Hotel, in Douglas.'

'You're a dark horse!' exclaimed Jane, 'You might have shared that with Katy and me over breakfast.'

'Yes,' apologised Simon, 'I should have, sorry. I was busy thinking about the inquest; it's tomorrow morning. Do you know who killed the Elliot guy, Raymond?'

'I'm afraid not,' Raymond replied, 'That is still a mystery.'

'But we did discover how he got in,' Raymond continued, 'In his pocket, the inspector found a specialised tool, the kind used by very experienced burglars to pick locks.'

* * * *

The inquest was as much as Simon had imagined. He was first to testify. He explained why he had been at the house and described finding the body. Inspector Johnson was called next, and his testimony included all that the Chief Constable had told Simon. The coroner decided to call Katy and asked her about the condition of the house when she'd left it. Katy explained about the call to Africa and the need to rent the house and eventually shut it up. He also asked her to explain about the sales and contract documents she had discovered. She was then asked what she knew of the persons who, along with her deceased brother, had signed the contract. Katy said the only other one she knew was David Kingston. Although she had met James Walters in Africa, she knew nothing about him, except that he was Simon's father.

A screen and projector were brought into the courtroom, and Jane was then called and asked to identify the person shown on the blown-up photograph projected onto the screen. Jane affirmed that the person in the photograph was her estranged husband, James Walters.

Several others were called to testify regarding David Kingston, but none knew of his present whereabouts.

Finally, a representative of the dead man's firm was called, but only to assure the court that the deceased had not been working for the company at the time of his death.

The coroner's decision was murder by person or persons unknown, and the inquest was closed.

Over dinner at the hotel that evening, Katy informed Simon that she would stay on the Isle of Man and engage a contractor to clean and redecorate her home.

'After all, my father was an earl,' she announced, 'I have inherited a title.' With a smile, she continued, 'You may call me Lady Katherine Galloway.'

Chapter 17 - Visitors

Simon let himself into his apartment. He felt tired, even exhausted. He had only dozed briefly on the plane from the Isle of Man to Glasgow, and again on the bus to Edinburgh.

Jane had elected to stay on the Isle of Man and help Katy settle back into her home. Although he found it difficult saying goodbye, Simon knew his duty lay in Scotland. He was, in a way, looking forward to church routine again, and having his mind occupied with things other than Africa and events on the Isle of Man.

The short sleep on the plane had done little to alleviate his tiredness. He looked at his bags but decided to unpack later. Collapsing onto the settee, Simon fell into a blissful sleep. When he awoke, it was dark. He looked at his watch; he had slept for almost six hours. The smell of what the Scots call *oxters* convinced him that a shower was next on the agenda.

He then phoned Graham and brought him up to date with recent events. They arranged to meet the following morning, not at the church premises, but at Graham's other office – the coffee shop! Unable to sleep, Simon worked into the wee hours of the morning, going over the paperwork borrowed from Katy. He finally gave up and fell asleep sometime after three.

Later that morning, he kept his appointment with Graham and, together, they worked out Simon's schedule for the week ahead, ending with Simon preaching the following Sunday morning.

For the next few weeks, it was business as usual for Simon, with work in the church and the community. Jane, meanwhile, kept him abreast of the goings-on at Kingsway.

She told him that Katy had the place contractually cleaned from top to bottom. Now, the decorators were in painting and papering. She said that Katy had been shopping and refurnished the house: living room, bedrooms, kitchen and laundry.

'Love you, too,' said Simon, ending the call from his mum. He looked up as the door to his office opened. It was Freda, one of the volunteer workers.

'There are a couple of folks here to see you,' she said, 'Shall I send them in?'

'Who are they?' asked Simon, 'Did they say?'

'No,' responded Freda, 'A man and a woman. They said they were friends from Africa.'

'Right,' said Simon, feeling quite excited, 'Send them in.'

Freda nodded and left. A few moments later, she was back, accompanied by two people whose presence brought a smile to Simon's face.

Simon greeted Jennifer and Alinani warmly, with a hug for Jennifer, and an African greeting for Alinani.

'Ah, you remembered,' said Alinani with a smile, 'But here in your country, I am Alan.'

Freda asked if anyone would like coffee, and all three responded in the affirmative with thanks.

'What brings you here?' Simon asked.

'As you say here, we are killing two birds with one stone,' replied Alan, 'But in this case, it was three.'

'You remember Joseph?' asked Jennifer.

Simon gave a wry smile, 'I remember his driving.'

'Well,' continued Jennifer, 'Alan managed to find a place for him to stay in Birmingham, and he has been accepted for a Geology course in the university there. So, we travelled over with him; that pleased his grandmother.'

'That is bird number one,' Alan explained, 'Bird number two was surprising you, and, we had hoped, Katy.'

'Katy is back on the Isle of Man,' Simon informed his friends, 'And doing great things to her old home, so my mother informs me. She is also there, helping Katy.'

'Oh!' said Jennifer, 'I had hoped she'd be here.'

'I'll call her later,' responded Simon, 'What's bird number three?'

'Ah!' said Alan, 'There is a mission conference starting the day after tomorrow in Glasgow. We hadn't planned to come over for that, but when Joseph was accepted for his course, well, we couldn't resist coming with him. His father had planned to accompany him, but I think, because of his work commitments, he was relieved when we volunteered our services.'

The door opened, and Freda appeared with coffee and biscuits.

'Thanks,' said Simon to Freda. He asked Jennifer, 'How long does the conference last?'

'Just for four days,' she replied, 'And then we have to return to Zambia. We can't afford any more time away.'

'Let me ring Katy and fill her in.'

'Hello Simon,' answered Katy, recognizing his number, 'How are things with you?'

'Hi, Katy,' replied Simon, 'Things are fine, but the reason I'm calling is to say that I have, sitting in my office, your friends Jennifer and Alinani, or Alan, as he wants to be called whilst here. I'll let you speak to Jennifer.'

Simon listened as Jennifer and Katy made plans to meet in Glasgow the following day.

Jennifer told Katy that the conference was in the Marion Centre, not far from the airport.

Arrangements made, Simon invited his two friends to lunch.

They ate at a café near the church and during the meal, Simon told Jennifer and Alan about his last visit to the Isle of Man.

Afterwards, he drove them to the bus station and prayed with them before his two friends boarded the bus for Glasgow.

* * * *

Katy told Jane about the proposed visit to Scotland but said she had misgivings with all the work going on at Kingston.

'Of course, you must go,' said Jane, 'I can follow your instructions and look after the work here, it's almost finished, anyway. There is just the lounge and snug to complete inside. Have you made up your mind about the stables?'

'Leave the stables till I get back,' replied Katy, 'I'll talk it over with you then.'

With that, Katy booked a flight from the Isle of Man to Glasgow leaving the following afternoon, and her accommodation and dinner at the Airport Hotel.

* * * *

At breakfast the following morning, Jane found a picture and an obituary when reading through the morning paper; Raymond Caley, the Isle of Man Chief Constable had died in hospital following a heart attack. She called Katy and showed her the article.

'Of course, you knew him from years ago,' remarked Katy.

'I did,' Jane answered, 'And his wife, Liz. Raymond and Liz were both Manx and were married here; they had one son, Jack. She and I met at one of her church coffee mornings. We became friendly and would meet up occasionally for coffee in Douglas and at her home. When Raymond was promoted to Sergeant, he transferred to Birmingham. Liz and I kept in touch for a while, but our correspondence petered out after about a year. I knew she was back on the island, but we were moving in different circles. I'll pay her a visit and pass on our condolences.'

Chapter 18 - Kidnap

Katy's flight was on schedule. Soon, she was settled into her hotel room. Later that evening, she met up with Jennifer and Alinani. They had a meal together and reminisced about Africa. Katy arranged to meet up with them the following evening and watched from the hotel doorway as her friends walked away. At the street corner, they turned and waved, then disappeared from her view. Katy decided to have another coffee before retiring, so she sat in the lounge and read the local paper. Later, she made her way to the lift, thinking she would phone Jane from her room. At her door, as she was about to insert the entrance card, she heard footsteps in the corridor. As Katy glanced up, she saw a face she recognised. Hands grabbed her roughly, and something was placed over her mouth. Realisation dawned on her just as she slipped into a dreamless unconsciousness.

Katy opened her eyes as consciousness returned to find she was in darkness. She realized that a blindfold covered her eyes and she was travelling in a vehicle. She couldn't move her hands or feet, and she couldn't even scream; something was covering her mouth. Before long, the movement stopped, and she felt herself being lifted, carried briefly and set down on a seat. A car engine started, and she was moving again – to what and to where she did not know. Fear engulfed her as she recalled her captor's face. It was the man who called himself Mr Equinox, but whom Katy knew as James Walters; Jane's husband and Simon's father.

Katy still felt groggy and nauseous, but still the vehicle's journey continued and, once again, Katy slept.

When she awoke again there was no movement. She felt dreadfully uncomfortable and tried to move her body. Suddenly, she was lifted and carried. A voice said, 'I have brought your case with me; wasn't I very thoughtful?'

She heard a door opening and she was carried forward once again. Her bearer set Katy on her feet, and the restraints and blindfold were removed. She blinked as the sudden light struck her eyes. Then, as focus returned, Katy saw the faces of her captors. The one she already knew was that of James Walters; the other was that of David Kingston.

'Now, Katy,' Walters spoke, 'We will leave you to clean yourself up.' He pointed to the bathroom and then to her case: 'You are eight floors up, and there's no one in either of the adjacent rooms. Just make yourself at home. I'll come back later with some tea and biscuits. That's all I can provide at present, but there'll be proper food in the morning. The effects of the anaesthetic are already wearing off, but it will still help you sleep. I'll explain why you are here in the morning.'

All this time, Kingston stood by the door with a leer on his face; he never spoke. The two men left the room. Katy wasn't surprised when, on trying the door, she found it to be locked. She walked to the window and looked out to a yard and a building with a brick wall gable. It was dark and when she glanced at her watch, she saw it was almost midnight. Katy showered and dried but didn't feel refreshed. Dressed in her night attire and still feeling scared and groggy, she lay on the bed, outside the covers. Exhaustion took over. She was almost asleep when she heard a knock on the door. It opened, and James Walters entered, carrying a tray with two biscuits and a cup of tea.

He set the tray on the bedside table and said, 'Paltry, but I hope you enjoy your supper. I'll see you in the morning.'

Then he was gone, leaving Katy with her thoughts. Ignoring the supper tray, she left the bed and fell on her knees in prayer. She asked God for strength and wisdom and prayed for His protection and peace. Her prayers over, Katy climbed back into bed – this time, under the covers. Once more, the feeling of exhaustion came over her, but it was strangely mingled with a deep feeling of peace, as some verses of scripture, verses she had learned at Sunday school, pervaded her mind.

One verse stood out from the others from Psalm 23:

'Yea, though I walk through the valley of the shadow of death, I will fear no evil; For You are with me; Your rod and Your staff, they comfort me.'

Leaving the tea and biscuits untouched, Katy drifted away to a place of dreams, and dream she did. Faces floated before her; mother smiled at her, dad said some cheering words, and Simon, Jane, Jennifer and Alinani were all there. Then, the leering face of David Kingston appeared, and she heard him say that she was for it, and she would go the same way as her brother.

Katy screamed!

There was a knock, and the door opened; it was James Walters carrying another, no, the same tray. Katy recognised the flower patterns on the edges.

'David looked in on you earlier this morning,' he said, 'And saw you hadn't touched the tea and biscuits. He didn't wake you, just took the tray away.'

'So,' thought Katy, 'His presence wasn't a dream. He had been here, and he'd said something about my brother.' She tried in vain to recall his words, but the memory escaped her. Katy wanted to rebel, but the toast and scrambled egg looked appetising, and she was hungry.

'Enjoy,' said Walters and left the room.

Katy had barely finished her breakfast when the door again opened. This time, it was Kingston who entered.

'I see you enjoyed your breakfast,' he said. Again, that leering voice and expression were present.

'You spoke to me during the night,' Katy accused, 'And said something about Joel.'

'Ah, poor Joel. You know, he was going to turn me in; he had a fit of conscience after everything I had done for that ungrateful brat. James plans to talk to you later, but I'll do some talking now. Joel had taken and hidden a certain document, which I needed. I met with him in the stables at your home on the morning he died. I asked Joel where it was, but he just looked at me and laughed and told me it was in a secret place. I didn't like that, so I found a piece of rope. At first, I considered tying him up and using the old cigarette-burn torture to make him talk, but I forgot I didn't smoke.'

He laughed again, but this time, it ended in a choke.

'So, you know what I did?'

The leer on his face had gone, and a strange look of sadness spread over his features, as though the memory of what he had done was difficult to bear.

In a much more subdued manner, David Kingston now vocalised the memory: 'I made the rope into a noose and put it around his neck. I threw the other end of the rope over a rafter and tied it to a roof support. He was still laughing, thinking this was some kind of joke. There was a crate nearby on the floor. I set it on its side and lifted Joel on to it. I said I would kick the crate away unless he told me where the document was. He stopped smiling. Then the silly fool struggled, trying to slacken the noose, and the crate fell over. I wanted to help him, but I panicked and hid when I heard voices outside, but they didn't come near the stables. When I went back to your brother, I knew by his face he was dead. I hadn't meant for him to die.'

When he spoke again, his voice was soft, his expression – almost frightened.

'You must believe me, Katy. I didn't mean for Joel to die. I was fond of the young whipper-snapper, but he shouldn't have turned. All he had to do was give me the blooming document.'

As Katy looked at David Kingston, she wanted to hate him for what he had done, but the relief of knowing that her brother had renounced his criminal intent and was not a conspirator brought a great feeling of relief. It also gladdened Katy's heart to know that Joel hadn't committed suicide – once more, she experienced that feeling of inward peace.

'But Katy,' Kingston broke into her reverie, 'We need a certain item, and we think you might have it. It's a sales receipt and where Walters and I are concerned, it's an incriminating document. Walters believes you have it, and he will not release you till you give it to him or tell us where we can find it.'

Just at that moment, James Walters entered the room. He had obviously been listening before opening the door, for he said, 'Well, it's said that confession is good for the soul, David.' But his eyes were fixed on Katy's face, 'What about it, Katy? Where is our much sought-after document?'

For a moment, she considered bluffing, but then, a profound sense of peace engulfed her. She began to speak, and her voice was strong and steady, 'Never mind the document. Accident or not, Mr Kingston, you are responsible for my brother's death, and, indirectly, for the death of my parents. And as for you, Mr Walters, you are an accessory after the fact.'

Before either of the two men could comment, Katy continued: 'So, here's the deal. I did find the item you want, and only I know where it is. So, you will take me to the airport, and when I am back on the Isle of Man, I will send the document to whatever address you give me.'

'Wow!' said Walters, applauding, 'Miss Katy Galloway QC. I wonder if I can trust you?'

'Trust her?' Kingston interrupted. The leering voice was back: 'You are surely joking. Maybe I should slap her around a little and convince her that we are not mugs.'

'No,' continued the other man, 'I'm curious. Where did you find the document? We searched Joel's room, and indeed your home, very thoroughly, but without success. And who, apart from you, has seen the paper?'

'Apart from me, only Simon and Jane—your abandoned family—and one other, but he is dead,' Katy answered, 'I am the only one who knows where to find the item. And as to where I discovered it, that is unimportant.'

Walters spoke again, 'All right I will trust you.' Then, ignoring Kingston's protests, he said, 'I'll do what you ask, but don't you dare double-cross me, young lady. I can always find you and your friends. You see, Katy, unlike my passionate friend here, I am not a violent person. My means of revenge are more business-like. I don't hurt the persons; I destroy their livelihoods. And I don't need to lift a finger; I just phone a contact.'

Katy forced herself not to smile, but again, in a steady voice, she said, 'Somehow, I don't think either of you will soon be in a position to extract any kind of revenge. I think your Mr Levinson has even more contacts, and from what I have learned of him, he will not take being conned out of five million dollars lying down.'

'Well, I think that proves you have the item we require, and once we have it, Jacob Levinson will be lying down, because he won't have a leg to stand on with regard to our deal.'

'Ha! Very good, James,' said Kingston with a laugh, 'But I think you are making a mistake in letting her go.'

'We'll see,' responded Walters, 'But now, Katy, pack your things. You are going home.'

Chapter 19 – Home

Jane phoned Simon at his office: 'Have you heard from Katy?'

'No. I thought she planned to travel home today.'

'I've tried her mobile,' said Jane, 'But it went to voicemail. Perhaps she is somewhere where she can't use her mobile. Are her friends still there?'

'No,' Simon answered, 'Jennifer and Alinani flew out this morning. They rang me and said that they were concerned because Katy didn't meet with them as planned and didn't answer her mobile. I wished them a safe flight and promised to let them know about Katy.'

Just then, his office phone rang; it was one of his parishioners. Simon's presence was urgently required and as he needed to attend to this request, he would ring his mum and Katy later.

****

At the airport, Katy purchased a flight to the Isle of Man, but not for that day; she booked it for two days hence. She then bought a SIM card at the airport O2 shop. When it was registered, she keyed the new number into her phone, then called Jane, hoping she was at Kingsway Mansion.

When she answered, Katy said, 'Jane, I'm on my phone at Glasgow airport, but with a new number

– long story. I want you, before you ask anything, to put my new mobile number into your system and text me Simon's number; I will be home in a couple of days, and then I will tell you everything, but right now, I need to phone Simon.'

When she finished her call, Katy looked around the terminal. She couldn't see either of her abductors, so she made her way to the coffee shop. There Katy spotted someone she recognised; it was a girl from the Isle of Man. Her name was Kirsty Quayle, and Katy had known her from high school; in fact, they had once been close friends.

As Katy approached, Kirsty looked up: 'Well, if it isn't Katy Galloway!' She exclaimed, 'I take it you are still a Galloway?' She glanced at Katy's bare fingers, 'Sit and have a coffee and catch-up.'

Katy told her a little of her days on the Isle of Man and in Africa, but nothing of the sinister circumstances.

'But tell me,' asked Katy, 'Are you still on the Isle of Man? I see you are married.'

'Yes, I am Mrs Jones now. My husband, as our name suggests, is from Wales; he is a Methodist minister on the island. I'm here to meet my sister. I'm sure you remember Charlotte; she was a class or two below us at college. She is working in Edinburgh but coming home for a holiday. I've flown over to meet her and do some shopping in Glasgow. Her bus isn't due for another half hour, so meeting you was advantageous.'

They chatted until it was time for Kirsty to leave and meet the Edinburgh bus. Another hug, a promise to keep in touch, and Kirsty left to meet her sister.

During their conversation, Katy's mobile had bleeped so she looked at it now, guessing it would be Jane, giving her Simon's number. Her guess was correct, and she dialled Simon's number.

'Where have you been and are you okay?' Simon asked once she'd identified herself.

'I'm at Glasgow Airport,' Katy replied, 'And I want to come and see you. I've spoken to your mum, and I will bring you my news when we meet. I need to visit the police station first and make a statement. I'll catch the bus and call when I am nearing Edinburgh. Can you pick me up?'

'Of course, I can,' he said, 'Mum and I were ringing your mobile, but it seemed to be switched off. After a few attempts, we got a bit concerned.'

'I will tell you everything when I see you,' Katy promised.

She took another good look around the airport terminal and decided it was safe to go then, hailing a taxi, Katy asked for the nearest police station.

At the police station, she spoke to the desk Sergeant and eventually to a detective. He listened to her story and asked her to put in writing.

'My friend in Edinburgh has a photo of one of my abductors which I will send to you,' said Katy and took her leave.

True to his word, Simon was waiting for her. As Katy approached the car, she burst into tears.

'Hey, there, there,' said Simon. He held Katy close before helping her into the car, 'I don't know what happened, but I assume you have been through the mill.'

On the journey into Edinburgh, Katy related her experiences and said she wanted to talk to Simon and Jane about her next step.

'I think you will have to keep your word about the sales document,' said Simon, 'I took a picture of it when mum and I first saw it, so we still have the evidence.'

'I take it you still have that photo of Mr Equinox?' asked Katy, 'Can I have it to give to the Glasgow police?'

'I'll look it out and send it with an explanatory note,' replied Simon, 'You have enough on your plate.'

'If you don't mind,' Katy asked, 'Can I stay in your mum's apartment? I just need some time to myself to think things through. I have a flight booked for the day after tomorrow. Could you then take me to Glasgow Airport? Oh, how I wish the Isle of Man flights still went from Edinburgh.'

* * * *

As she alighted from the plane, Katy was pleased to find herself on home territory. The last few days had been frightening, but exciting. She was still in one piece and had learned plenty, especially about Joel. She was still desperately sad about his death but gladdened by his obedience to conscience. Jane had arranged to pick her up at the airport and true to her word, she was waiting.

As she and Jane toured the refurbished Kingsway Mansion rooms, they chatted as they walked. Jane frowned as Katy related the events of the past days.

'Not to worry,' said Katy, 'I'm home, safe and sound. And the old house looks beautiful. I'm ready now for my next adventure.'

'Your next adventure?' Jane queried, 'Are you going back to Africa?'

'No,' replied Katy, 'I have written to Mr Kabaghe in Tanzania and asked him to accept my resignation, effective immediately. I know he has someone temporary in my post and perhaps she or he will take the job permanently. Anyway, whatever the outcome, I am home for good.'

'What about our two villains?' asked Jane, 'Are you going ahead with your promise?'

'Oh, yes,' replied Katy, 'I'll go and fetch their accursed document.'

For reasons of security, she had returned the sales document to her secret hideout in the stables. As she retrieved it, a wave of sadness swept over her, and tears started to flow. Katy allowed herself the comfort of crying, as memories of Joel came flooding back. Through her tears, she smiled, as she recalled the happy game-play she and Joel had enjoyed here throughout their childhood years.

Funny, she thought, we had never shared this secret place with Simon. And she, for the first time, wondered why.

Drying her tears, Katy collected the document, walked back to the house, sealed it in a large brown envelope and, with a smile, addressed it to Mr Equinox to the address Walters gave her. Then she left what she now called the accursed document on the hall table to post. She gave a wry smile as the term 'the accursed' came to mind. She recalled the man, Achan, in the Old Testament story of Joshua and the conquering of Jericho. Katy went to her room, opened her Bible and searched for the relevant passage of scripture. She read out loud to herself from Joshua, Chapter 7:

'But the children of Israel committed a trespass regarding the accursed things, for Achan the son of Carmi, the son of Zabdi, the son of Zerah, of the tribe of Judah,

took of the accursed things; so the anger of the Lord burned against the children of Israel.'

Katy fell on her knees and prayed a long and heartfelt prayer to God, seeking an end to her involvement with Walters and Kingston. She even found herself praying for them, that they might not end up like Achan in the Jericho story.

Chapter 20 – Kingsway

Over dinner, Katy and Jane talked about the future.

'Now that the work in the house is complete, I need to return to my life in Edinburgh,' said Jane, 'Although I did enjoy catching up with island events and past friends.'

'Then why go?' asked Katy, 'Go for good, I mean. After looking around my home I couldn't help thinking about converting Kingsway Mansion into a guest house. Of course, I couldn't manage it on my own, and I can't think of anyone else I'd rather have to help me than you.'

Jane stared at Katy for a while before speaking: 'I'll certainly give your proposal some earnest consideration, Katy. I will go home tomorrow and talk it over with Simon. Oh, so much to think about, Katy Galloway, and I do love you, just as I did when you, Joel and Simon were growing up here!'

Spontaneously, they both rose and hugged each other, and once again, tears flowed. In the afternoon, Jane packed her bags and booked the following morning's flight to Glasgow.

Katy and Jane talked well into the evening and prayed for each other. By the time they said good night, Jane had already made up her mind regarding her future.

* * * *

On the plane the next morning, Jane thought again of the decision she had made, but not yet shared with Katy.

Jane had prayerfully decided that her future lay on the Isle of Man and with Katy. She wondered what Simon would say when she told him. She enjoyed the journey by bus to Edinburgh and cab to her home.

Once inside her apartment, Jane put the kettle on, then phoned a surprised Simon and invited him for lunch. Next Jane phoned Katy and told her she'd had an uneventful journey. She still didn't say anything to Katy about her decision. She had unpacked, prepared a meal and had a short sleep by the time she heard Simon's key in the door.

'I missed you so much!' he declared, giving her a bearlike hug.

During their meal, Jane told Simon of Katy's plan and of her decision to move back to the Isle of Man.

'Why am I not surprised?' asked Simon, 'I can already visualise you and Katy entertaining guests in that big house.'

They both laughed, then Jane asked, 'What should I do about the apartment? Should I sell?'

'I think that, also, would be a wise decision,' Simon answered, 'I, too, am having a change of direction. The church wants me to pastor a new church-plant planned for Kinross. I will go there, God willing, in September.'

'Oh, Simon, pastor of your own church, that is such wonderful news!' exclaimed Jane and gave him another hug.

'Meanwhile, will you look after the sale of the apartment for me?' Jane asked, 'I feel the need to return to the island as soon as possible.'

'My pleasure,' answered Simon, 'When do you plan to go back?'

'ASAP,' replied Jane: 'In fact, probably tomorrow, if you don't mind.'

'Why should I mind?' responded Simon, 'You are your own boss.'

She admitted to herself that she was quite excited at the prospect of turning Kingsway Mansion into a B&B.

* * * *

With Jane away, Kate decided to make a start on the stables.

'No good me trying to do the curtains,' she thought to herself. 'I wouldn't know where to start!'

As she passed the garage a thought entered Katy's mind: her father's car had gone to auction but... taking her keys from her pocket, Katie hurried to the garage and unlocked the doors. Pulling them open, to her delight, she gazed upon her mother's Toyota Corolla. Katy remembered she had bought it new, just a year before the tragedy, so the car was really only a year old. Rubbing the dust from the side window Katy read the mileage: 1500. One of her keys opened the box on the garage wall where Katy knew her mum kept a spare key. She opened the car door and from the back seat took out a rug which she shook violently, choking on the dust. Katy then laid the rug on the driver's seat and located the key in the ignition. Hopefully, she turned the key but no response. She phoned the Toyota garage in Ramsey, explained the situation and gave her name and mobile number. The helpful receptionist told her that she was sure the garage could help and someone would ring her back. Katy meanwhile brought the vacuum cleaner, cloths and polish from the house and began a 'spring clean' inside and outside. Her mobile rang and when she answered, a man's voice said, 'Hello, am I speaking to Katy Galloway?' When Katy responded in the affirmative he continued, 'best if we collect your car and tow it to the garage; the engine at least will need a good going over. One of our mechanics, Jimmy, will call with you in about half-an-hour. Could I have your address please?'

Katy thanked him and gave her address. True to their word the company tow truck arrived inside the given time and a young man whom Katy supposed was Jimmy approached her.

'Thank you for being so prompt,' Katy said and pointed to the garage. 'The car is in there.'

'Righto,' responded Jimmy and, climbing back into his cab, reversed the tow-truck up to the garage door. After lifting the bonnet and looking at the engine, he climbed back into his cab. 'The garage will call you when the car is ready,' he called, 'it shouldn't take too long.'

Katy waved goodbye as Jimmy, tow-truck and Toyota headed towards Ramsey. Katy then phoned for a taxi and at the post office, gladly paid the postage and watched, with a sense of relief, as the cashier dropped the envelope into the post bag.

On closer examination, Katy could see that the work required to make the stables into something habitable would take stronger arms than hers. As if in answer to an unspoken prayer, a Manx Telecom van entered the drive. Katy knew the driver would be Jonathan Quayle, a Manx Telecom engineer. He had been in Simon's class at school, and Katy had sometimes met with him and his wife in Ramsey while shopping.

'Hi, Katy,' Jonathan called, as Katy emerged from the stables. 'Put the kettle on; I'm dying for a cup of tea.'

'Hello, Jonathan,' responded Katy, 'Come on into the kitchen.'

Over tea and scones—baked by Jane, not her—Katy asked after Joanne and their little girl.

'Not so little now,' Jonathan answered, 'She's eighteen months and just starting to walk. Joanne is doing great; she's back at work part-time, and her mum looks after Louise for two days a week. I work flexi hours, so I can take care of her for the third day. But, what about your plans?'

'I have decided to stay on the island,' answered Katy, 'And I am hoping to open up the house, and possibly the stables, like a B&B. Jane—I'm sure you remember Simon's mum—has been over here helping me.'

'I saw Simon not so long ago, here on the island. Didn't get a chance to speak to him; I was up a telegraph pole at the time.'

'Jane is over in Scotland with Simon at the moment,' said Katy, 'He is in ministry, working with a church in Edinburgh.'

'Good for Simon! We in his class always thought he was 'good living,' said Jonathan with a smile, 'But what about these stables? I could round up a few friends; I'm sure it wouldn't take long to do a clear out. Let's take a look.'

Once inside, Jonathan said, 'Look's a bigger job than I thought but leave it with me. I'll give you a call later in the week. Now, must get on. Thanks for the tea; it was a godsend.'

'Oh no, Jonathan,' Katy thought to herself, 'You were the godsend.' Out loud, she said: 'Love to Joanne and give Louise a cuddle from me. And say *hello* to your mum. When Jane returns, we'll have her and your dad over for dinner.'

As Jonathan drove off, Katy decided she would make a start on clearing out the smaller items in the stable. While she toiled, her mind worked furiously as well. How many bedrooms could she have? What about the kitchen; would it need to be upgraded? And parking? She would need most of the rear lawn removed and a driveway built to the rear of the house. She stopped working and sat down, feeling a little dejected. Even with volunteer help, the change around would cost a small fortune. Katy decided to leave what she was doing, have a shower and go to the pictures.

She liked Gene Hackman and was pleased to see the picture of the day was *The Runaway Jury*. Katy remembered reading the book by John Grisham and was a little disappointed that the plot was about guns, whereas the book was about cigarettes. However, she enjoyed the movie, even though Gene Hackman played the bad guy.

Just then the phone rang; it was the Ramsey garage receptionist to say that the mechanic had finished checking the car and, apart from an oil change and battery charge and clean-up, the car was ready for collection. Katy responded that she would pick it up within the hour. She was pleased to hear the cost was minimal and phoned for a taxi to come straight away. At the garage Katy paid the bill and gazed with admiration at a clean Toyota Corolla. Climbing into the driving seat she turned the ignition key and, delighted, drove out of the garage towards Douglas.

She didn't go straight home after the picture, but treated herself to a meal at the Mandarin, a Chinese restaurant with a good reputation.

During the meal, Katy received a text from Jane to say she was booked on the five o'clock flight.

Katy responded with 'look forward to seeing you and I have a surprise to show you.' She then paid her bill and drove home.

At seven o'clock Katy, on the lookout, saw Jane's car enter the driveway and, opening the front door, she walked over and leaned on her Toyota.

As Jane got out of her car she asked, 'What's this? You bought a new car?'

'No,' laughed Katy, 'I found it. This is my mum's car and it had sat in the garage for last six or seven years. I had forgotten all about it and had the Ramsey garage check it over. It's going great.'

In the kitchen over a cup of tea Jane told Katy of her decision to stay on the island and partner her in the plans for the B&B.

Katy rose from the table and wrapped Jane in a hug. 'Oh, you have no idea how pleased this makes me feel. *Katy and Jane* or *Jane and Katy* – partners in business. I have some good news, too; I had word from our architect that the proposed plans for the house and stables are ready. He wants me, now us, to view them tomorrow.'

The following morning, Katy and Jane visited the architect's office in Ramsey and looked with astonishment and delight at the proposed plan. The house could support five bedrooms, all en suite, and the proposed plan showed the conversion of the stable into two self-catering cottages. The architect also gave them the news that he was confident the planning department would pass his plans.

The two ladies stopped for lunch at the Northern Hotel, then drove home, excited about the future. They received quite a surprise when, entering the driveway to the house, they saw three cars already parked there.

As they walked around to the stables, they found Jonathan with two men whom Katy recognised as former schoolmates, Keith Watson and Garry Manson. The three were carrying lots of bulky items from the stables and piling them on the grass.

On seeing Katy, Jonathan called out, 'Hi there, Katy. I called at the house earlier to ask about starting the clear out. I talked with Keith and Garry yesterday, and they were both available today, so I just went ahead and phoned them. I hope you don't mind us making a start without your permission.'

'Mind?' said Katy, 'I am delighted. Hello, Keith and Garry; long time, no see!'

She introduced Jane, and they chatted about old times, Simon and the future. Katy then told them to go ahead and pull everything out and asked Jonathan to hire a skip in her name. The three men said they would return on Saturday morning and fill the skip. They agreed that Katy should decide what else needed doing and draw up a job list. Apart from a break for refreshments, which Jane provided, all five worked through the afternoon and ended the day pleased with the result. The three men had a wash at the house, refused to stay for refreshments, and drove away, leaving an excited Jane and Katy to discuss the house plans.

They walked around the house, looking into all the rooms and trying to envisage the end result. Then, quite exhausted, they both had an early night.

Chapter 21 – Manchester

A courier picked up the package from the London box office address and sent it, as instructed, to his company's Manchester office. The company van pulled up outside an apartment block in Barlow Moor Road, Chorlton Cum Hardy, Manchester. Receiving no answer to his ring, he tried the second apartment. The occupant of number two was an ex-army officer named John Watkins. Wounded during a spell in Iraq and invalided out of his regiment, the former Major John Watkins was finding it difficult to come to terms with civilian life. Formerly from London, he'd decided, after his demob from the army, to move to Manchester, far away from his ex-wife, but close to his daughter, who lived and worked there. John was sitting at his kitchen table, looking at the raindrops meandering down the window and dreaming of what might have been when a buzz from the door intercom shook him from his reverie.

Pressing the acknowledgement button, John answered, 'Yes?'

'Sorry to disturb you, sir. I have a large envelope for your neighbour at number four, a Mr Equinox, but there is no answer from his apartment. I wonder, would you collect it, please? It needs a signature.'

'Yes, of course,' John replied. He used the stairs. Since he lived on the first floor, he always found it quicker to take the stairs than to wait for the lift. Arriving in the lobby, John opened the door and signed for the envelope.

'Much obliged,' said the courier, as he handed the package to John.

John knew the occupants on his floor but had only met the occupant of number four a few times, and even then, it was just to say hello. Something at the back of his mind told him that he had heard his neighbour's name spoken once before, but he couldn't remember when. One thing he did remember, however, was that it hadn't been *Mr Equinox*.

'What an unusual name. Probably fictitious, or the envelope could be for someone else and not for my neighbour at all.' As he turned towards the lobby letter boxes, John saw that he couldn't post the envelope; his neighbour's post box was already full, and the postman had even left two letters sitting on the floor. John picked them up and saw that the name on all the other envelopes was *Mr James Walters*. He brought the three envelopes via the stairs to his floor and knocked on the door of apartment four but received no answer. Then, John heard his own telephone ringing and quickly entered his apartment.

The caller was his daughter, Millie.

'Hello, Dad,' she said, 'I need your help. Your lovely little granddaughter is ill. The school phoned me at work, and I collected her. It seems like she has quite a high temperature, so I've called the doctor. Would you come round and take care of her until the doctor comes? I need to get back to work.'

'It would be my pleasure,' replied John, 'Tell Emily I'm on my way.'

Placing the envelopes on his hall table, he quickly donned his coat and left to look after his only, and beloved, granddaughter, Emily.

Later that evening, having made sure that Millie could manage without him, John returned to his apartment. Only when he entered did he remember the envelopes. John picked them up and went next door. He knocked, but there was no reply. Wondering if there might be a window open, he returned to his apartment and opened his emergency exit door. Walking along the platform, he could see there was an open window. But as he approached, John noticed flies – and more than the usual number for an August evening. Then he noticed the smell!

In his army days, Major John Watkins had entered many houses after an enemy raid, and he knew the smell of decaying corpses. Standing outside his neighbour's window, he recognised that smell. Putting his handkerchief to his mouth and nose, John peered in through the open window. Flies were buzzing everywhere, but especially around the figure lying sprawled on a kitchen chair, his sightless eyes staring at the ceiling. John noticed that the hands and feet of the corpse were tied to the chair and there was a gag in his mouth.

Touching nothing, he returned to his apartment and dialled 999. John gave the policeman details of what he had discovered and was asked to admit the police when they arrived. He realised he was still holding the envelopes.

When his buzzer sounded, John admitted the police into the apartment block and waited while they ascended to his floor. The lift door opened, and two officers stepped out, male and female.

John quickly introduced himself.

The female officer thanked John and asked, 'Who has a key to the apartment; do you know?'

'The management company, I should think,' answered John, 'I'll get you their number.'

John found it and gave it to her, then more police arrived and cordoned off the landing and the stairs.

'Don't leave the building, please,' the Sergeant said, 'I will need to speak with you later. And when you do need to go out, use the emergency exit.'

John nodded and re-entered his apartment, where he poured himself a whisky – the second since his discovery. He knew better than to offer any to the police team but sat and waited for the next move. Before long, he heard voices outside and recognised that of the apartment manager.

'We just need your key, sir,' he heard the Constable say to the manager, 'No one can enter at present. I'll take the key, please.'

When the manager, with lots of questions, eventually obliged, the Constable escorted him to the lift.

'All entrances will be sealed and manned,' the Constable said just before the lift doors closed on the departing manager.

* * * *

The officer called in to take charge of the investigation was DCI Jack Caley; he was drafted in from Salford to take over the case. The station Superintendent, Bill Richards, felt this was a job for a Detective Chief Inspector.

DCI Caley and his Sergeant, Ms Lesley Connor, and another policeman, both well experienced in this kind of investigation, accompanied him to the crime scene.

The Constable guarding the landing handed the key to the DCI and resumed his position at the top of the stairs. As Jack opened the door, he and his Sergeant recognised the pungent odour that often accompanied this kind of investigation.

Clothed in the usual white overalls, mask, boots and gloves, they entered the apartment. Even though they quickly closed the door behind them, the duty Constable gagged at the escaping smell.

The two investigators took in the gruesome scene.

'I think we will leave this to forensics and to the scene of crime officer,' said Caley through his mask, 'We can look in again after they've finished.'

He suggested his Sergeant speak to the man who had discovered the body.

'I'll get some fresh air,' said Jack, 'And I'll meet you back at the station.'

He stripped off his protective gear, washed, and left the building.

Connor stripped off her protective gear and bagged it. She too washed, sprayed herself with a deodorant and knocked on John Watkins' door. After he admitted her, she introduced herself.

'Mr Watkins,' she said, 'My name is Police Sergeant Connor. While the SOCO team are upstairs we need to talk.'

With a puzzled expression on his face, John asked, 'Who or what is soco?'

'S-O-C-O,' Sergeant Connor explained, 'Stands for the Scene of Crime Officer. He or she is an officer who gathers forensic evidence for the police – well, the British police. They are known by different names in other countries. SOCOs are usually not police officers but are employed by the police force. The evidence collected is passed to the detectives in charge of the case and to forensic laboratories.'

'Ah! CSI,' remarked an enlightened John.

'Well,' responded Connor, with a smile, 'Don't believe all you see on television.'

'As you said on the phone,' she continued, 'There's something not right next door.'

'As a former army officer, I know death and decay when I smell it,' John replied and handed the envelopes to the Sergeant, 'I collected these for my neighbour and was trying to deliver them when I found the corpse.'

The Sergeant took the envelopes and then asked him to go through the events of the day.

Starting with the courier's arrival, John related everything that had occurred. She had just finished her notes and put her notebook away when there was a knock at the door. John admitted the lobby Constable.

'We're gathering quite a crowd at the entrance,' he said, 'I knocked on the doors of the other two apartments but got no answer.'

'No,' said John, 'They work during the day. They are probably wondering why they can't get into their homes.'

'Probably right,' said the Sergeant. As she and the Constable walked into the hall, Connor turned to John and said, 'Thanks for your help; you've done everything right. I'll take the envelopes with me and have them fingerprinted. I'll talk with you again later.'

Once out on the landing, the Sergeant called the Constable guarding the entrance: 'Find out if any occupants are there and admit them.'

A few moments later, the lift door opened, and two couples exited. Connor asked for their apartment numbers then said:

'Once inside your apartments, please don't try to leave via either exit until our forensic team have completed their investigations – that will probably be well into the night. Sorry for the inconvenience. If you wish, you can gather up some belongings and leave now, before they commence.'

They informed her that they would remain in their apartments.

* * * *

In apartment number four, two of the three members of the SOCO team, properly kitted out, commenced their examination. In the kitchen, they found the decaying corpse, whom they assumed was the occupant. On further investigation, though, the team soon knew the death was not due to natural causes. The body was, as the informant had described, sprawled in a chair, tied and gagged. One of the team cut the ties, and then, as a detailed examination began, another member recorded everything on camera. Once finished, they had the body placed in a body bag.

Before they removed the body, the police Constable told the folks gathered on the stairs to return to their homes, as they could well be contaminating a crime scene. The forensic team had already jammed the lift door open, so no one could use it. Eventually, two team members exited the apartment, carrying the body bag, and entered the lift. They reached the ground floor and found that the entrance was cordoned off, and a Constable was standing guard. He raised the cordon ribbon and allowed the members of the forensics team to leave. Once the body bag was in their wagon, they removed their protective clothing and drove away.

Connor gave the Constable instructions regarding the crime scene, assured him he would be relieved later and made her exit.

The third SOCO member remained behind, examining not only the apartment but also the surrounding exit area. Searches began in the landing, lift and fire escape. Various pieces of what might be evidence were collected and bagged. The work continued well into the night, but, when John opened his door the following morning, only the apartment was cordoned off; there was no sign of police. Deciding it was safe to leave the building by the conventional route, he started down the stairs. The lobby, too, was empty of police; people were coming in and going out as normal. John, too, felt almost normal as he left and headed for the newsagents to buy his usual *Daily Mail*.

* * * *

Chapter 22 - Investigation

In his new, and hopefully temporary, office, DCI Jack Caley and Sergeant Connor began sorting through the material on the desk. The name on most of the envelopes was *Mr James Walters*. Jack paused and considered the name. It rang a bell – he had known a Mrs Walters when he was young.

Now that his boys were grown up and in high school, their visits to the island were less frequent. Of course, the family's recent visit had been to attend his father's funeral. His mum had been pleased to see him and Laura, but especially happy to see their two boys.

Jack remembered the delight on the face of his dad when, after university, Jack had told him he would enrol in the police force.

'Education is so important,' he had said upon learning of Jack's promotion from Sergeant to an Inspector, 'I came up the hard way.'

Jack remembered his dad, studying into the wee small hours, determined to reach his goal. He did better than that, surprising his peers by becoming the youngest Chief Constable in the Birmingham division. By that time, Jack, himself married with two children, had moved to Manchester and passed his inspector course. Now, he was a chief inspector – 'Oh, how swiftly the years have flown,' he thought to himself, 'I'll have to visit more often; mum must be very lonely.'

He knew that both his parents had families on the island, and they were sure to call occasionally.

Jack shook himself out of his reverie when Connor spoke:

'This is from the large brown envelope addressed to Mr Equinox,' she said handing Jack a single document, 'It appears to be a sales contract and a property report, and the envelope has an Isle of Man postmark.'

He frowned as he read the document: 'The Plain of Ayre,' he read aloud. The only Ayre he knew of on the Isle of Man was the Point of Ayre, where he and his dad had often walked and where his children loved to play.

Jake Brisco, one of the SOCO team, called to report that they had managed to obtain a clear fingerprint from the corpse but had found no match on record.

After disconnecting, he examined the other mail, some of which concerned a business in Africa. One document had to do with the apartment and another envelope contained a cryptic note which was signed *The Other Mr Equinox*. It mentioned '*the item from the Isle of Man*', and asked a question: '*Did he have it?*' The envelope had an Isle of Man postmark.

Jack wondered if the item mentioned in the note could be the sales document. As he scanned the sales document, Jack saw the name James Walters signed as a director of the Isle of Man Property Company. It seemed very likely that dead man was James Walters. The Isle of Man connection seemed relevant and the name Walters familiar. It was starting to come back to him. He was sure that he had met a Mrs Walters on one of his visits to the Isle of Man. She used to visit his home when he was a boy and he remembered her writing to his mother after they moved to Birmingham. Dare he put two and two together?

If the corpse was James Walters, and Mrs Walters still lived on the Isle of Man then perhaps she could help. But he would have to tread carefully. First, Jack phoned his mum to ask if Mrs Walters still lived on the island and, if so, how could he get in touch.

'She is still here and living in Katy Galloway's house,' his mum replied, 'She visited me recently and said I should call her if I ever needed company. It's a mobile number; would you like me to text it to you?'

'Hark at you, all technical. No, just read it out,' replied Jack. He copied the dictated number into his mobile phone contacts.

'Thanks, mum. How are you keeping?' he asked.

'Oh, I am mentally, emotionally and physically stronger than most people think, even you,' his mum answered, 'But I would like to see you and the family before school begins if that is possible.'

'We will do our best; I'll get Laura to ring this evening,' said Jack. 'Talk it over with her. Look after yourself, Mum, and thanks. Hope to see you soon. Goodbye.'

Jack couldn't remember a Katy Galloway but remembered a Lord and Lady Galloway who lived in the north of the island.

Jack then dialled the mobile number his mum had given him.

'Hello. Jane Walters here.'

'Mrs Walters, this is Jack Caley, son of the late Chief Constable. I believe you knew each other,' Jack said.

'Yes, indeed,' Jane replied, 'I visited your mother shortly after your father's funeral. I was saddened by his death; he and I were helping to solve a mystery concerning my young friend, Katy Galloway.'

'Interesting,' said Jack, 'Katy Galloway? Is she related to Joel Galloway?'

'Oh, yes, he was her brother. Why do you ask?'

'Never mind that, now. I need your help,' said Jack, 'Your husband, James – do you know where he is?'

Jane replied, 'London, I think. About a week or so ago, Katy sent an envelope to him at a box office address there.'

'A large brown one?' asked Jack.

'Yes,' came the surprised reply.

'I have it. Apparently, a courier delivered it to an apartment here in Manchester. I believe your husband lived here. We are trying to trace him and would like to compare his fingerprints with ones found in the apartment. I wondered if you had anything belonging to your husband from which we could lift his prints.'

'My dear boy, my husband left me over twenty years ago, so I have nothing belonging to him, sorry. Oh wait, he touched Katy's camera in Africa and I don't think Katy has touched it much since she came home. If she is willing, I could have her wrap it carefully and send it to you.'

'No, don't do that,' Jack countered, 'I'll chat with police on the island and have them pick it up. Meanwhile, talk to Katy, but don't either of you touch it. And thanks for calling in with mum and offering her your friendship. Goodbye.'

Jack left the office and spoke to the desk Sergeant.

'Sorry, I don't know your name,' he began.

'Sergeant Ken Wilkes, sir,' came the response.

'Thanks, Ken. I need to get in touch with a detective on the Isle of Man. Have you any contacts there?'

'I knew your father, sir. He was here at conferences, and sometimes on investigations. I remember, on one occasion, he had a young detective with him. I can see his face. Give me a minute.'

Sergeant Wilkes closed his eyes, as if in meditation, before speaking again: 'Lewis. Yes, Detective Lewis. Sorry, sir, the brain's not as quick as it used to be. I'm due for retirement in a few months.'

'Thanks, Ken,' said Jack, 'Would you see if he is still on the force, and ask him, or perhaps another detective, to call me?'

A short time later Jack's phone rang. It was DI Lewis from the Isle of Man Police Station. After introductions and commiserations regarding Jack's father, Jack gave DI Lewis an update on the dead man whom he thought might be a Jack Walters.

'Mrs Walters who lives at Kingsway Mansion, the home of the late Lord and Lady Galloway, has a camera which may have our corpse's finger prints on it. I'd appreciate it if you could pick up the camera and send it to me.'

He heard DI Lewis laugh, then the reply, 'I assure the camera will be picked up and any fingerprints transmitted electronically to your computer. All I need is your e mail address.'

Jack obliged and after some further police conversation, ended the call.

* * * *

'I believe the dead man is, or was James Walters,' Jack said to Connor, 'I'm waiting for confirmation from the Isle of Man police. Apparently, Walters handled a camera, and his prints may still be on it. The Isle of

Man police will send them to SOCO who got a reasonably good fingerprint from the corpse.'

DCI Caley and Sergeant Connor examined the rest of the mail.

'See what information you can get from these African letters. Try and find out what Mr Walters was up to there,' Jack instructed his Sergeant, 'I'll follow up on this sales document. I think my informant may be one Katy Galloway. It is her camera the island police are, hopefully, picking up.'

Sergeant Connor went to her office and began making phone calls. A Sergeant of long experience, she knew how to acquire information from home and abroad. The letters were very cryptic; they avoided complete addresses and phone numbers, but one letter had enough information to cause her to make a phone call to a former colleague, now working with the police in Botswana. It took a while but eventually, she managed to track him down. His name was Nick Lassiter, and he had worked for some years with the fraud squad. She remembered, with a wry smile, that they had dated a few times, but only casually. Connor rang his number. She knew he'd been promoted after his secondment to the police force in Botswana, but she didn't know his present rank.

'Hello.'

'Hello, Nick,' she answered, 'Lesley Connor here.'

'Well, blow me down! How did you find me?' he asked.

'Ah, I'm a Detective Sergeant now, Nick. A veritable female Sherlock Holmes,' Lesley Conner replied with a laugh, 'And what about you?'

'I'm now a DI and involved mainly in cases involving Europeans,' he answered, 'But, I assume this is not a social call; what can I do for you, Lesley?'

'I'm involved in a murder case here in Manchester. We think the victim is one James Walters and that he has links with Africa. One letter we found and a witness, suggests he was in Botswana at one time. He also seems to use the name Mr Equinox,' replied Lesley.

'Aha! Now, you have just struck a chord,' said Nick, 'That name was part of an investigation about a year ago. I wasn't involved, but because I was from England, the local fraud squad asked me if I had come across that name. Apparently, it had something to do with property sales in districts of Africa, but, as far as I recall, mainly here in Botswana and Nigeria. Leave it to me, and I will make enquiries. Meanwhile, Detective Sergeant Connor, what else is exciting in your life?'

Sergeant Connor spent some time updating Nick on her life outside of the police, and they finally agreed to keep in touch. They exchanged phone numbers, both for personal and business purposes, and finally, the call ended.

Later that afternoon, Nick informed Lesley that Equinox was a company, now defunct, involved in fraudulent property deals. The Nigerian police had the directors' names on their wanted list. The company had offices in Lagos, but he was told that, when checked, the address turned out to be an empty shop in the city's Broad Street. Nick said he would email Lesley the names of the directors. Two were African and two were English. There was another name, listed as an associate, which was also English.

Lesley thanked Nick and again promised to keep in touch. A few minutes later, the names appeared in Lesley's email inbox. She headed to DCI Caley's borrowed office and picked up two coffees on the way. The DCI was on the phone, so he motioned her to sit and mouthed *thank you* for the coffee.

'Thank you, sir,' said Jack and ended the call: 'That was our super looking for an update,' he told Lesley.

Jack took a long drink of his coffee and then brought his Sergeant up to date, 'If the fingerprints on the camera match the print of our dead man we will know he was James Walters. So, what have you learned?'

Sergeant Connor told him of her breakthrough from one of the letters and of her conversation with, and subsequent information from her former colleague, Nick.

She had written the names of the directors and associate on a page from her notepad and presented it to her DCI.

'Victor Oluwaseyi,' read Jack, 'Awale Adebayo, and there's James Walters and another Englishman, David Kingston. Do we know anything about him?'

'Not yet,' said Sergeant Connor, 'I'm not sure where to start.'

'I would call this number,' said Jack, writing it on his notepad, 'DI John Lewis is a detective on the Isle of Man, and our mysterious document has Isle of Man connections.'

'Ah,' he read from her paper, 'Joel Galloway. There certainly is an Isle of Man connection. I think I need to speak to Mrs Walters again.'

'Right, sir,' said Sergeant Connor, 'I will phone the Isle of Man and talk with DI Lewis. His name is familiar.'

'Chat with Sergeant Wilkes,' advised Jack, 'He gave me his name, said he met him as a young detective. He was here with my father at a police conference.'

'Your father, sir?' enquired Sergeant Connor.

'Oh, yes, he was the Chief Constable on the Isle of Man. In fact, I was born there; he passed away a short while ago.'

'Oh, I'm sorry, sir,' said his Sergeant, 'I'll chat with Sergeant Wilkes.'

At the office door, she turned and said, 'The Isle of Man seems to figure a lot in this investigation. I've never been there. Would the budget run to my paying the island a visit?'

'Do you know, Connor,' answered the DCI, 'I think that would be an excellent idea. I'll get back to you when I've chatted to Mrs Walters.'

'Thank you, sir,' Sergeant Connor said, and she left to speak with Sergeant Wilkes.

Chapter 23 - Suspicions

Jane received a call from the police to say that someone would call and pick up the camera (Katy had left for another meeting with her architect and gave her permission to hand over the camera). Jane told the police she would pass it on to the messenger. Within the hour, a police car arrived at Katy's home and, with great care, a Constable transferred the camera from Katy's shoulder bag to an evidence bag.

When Katy returned from her visit, she updated Jane on the progress with the apartment and learned that the camera had been picked up. Jane told her about her conversation with DCI Jack Caley and mentioned that he was the son of the late Chief Constable.

'Let's talk no more today,' said Katy, 'We'll put a fire on in the lounge, sit back with our feet up and watch a DVD.'

And that is what they both did.

The following morning, Jane looked up from adjusting a curtain frill and saw a white van pull into the driveway. It stopped at the front door, and a man alighted from the passenger side and stopped, as though to survey the house, before approaching the door. Jane called to Katy, who was in the snug, 'Katy, you've got a visitor.'

The doorbell rang as Katy emerged from the snug, which she had turned into an office. She looked at Jane, who shrugged and shook her head. She opened the door.

The man standing there greeted her with a smile.

'Good afternoon, Miss Galloway?'

'A greeting and a question,' thought Katy.

'Good afternoon,' she replied, 'And yes, I am Miss Galloway.'

'Oh, good! I wasn't sure if I had the right address,' the man said, 'I am here to collect a package for a...' he paused to look at his notebook, 'Mr Walters.'

Katy was immediately suspicious. Remembering what Jane had told her, Katy's eyebrows wrinkled in a frown.

Regaining her composure, she said, 'Just a moment. I think I know where it is.'

Retreating into the hallway, she went to her office and searched for a large envelope. Finding one, she inserted two knitting patterns she had been looking at when Jane called. Katy sealed the envelope and scribbled *James Walters* on the front. When she returned to the waiting courier, she handed him the envelope and said, 'Here you are. Do you know where to take it? He didn't give me an address.'

'We have our instructions. Thank you, miss. Good day.'

Jane watched from the window as the man got into the van. As far as she could tell, he didn't open the envelope.

'What on earth did you give him?' she asked, as Katy entered the room.

'Just an envelope with two knitting patterns inside,' replied Katy, suppressing a laugh, 'Did you see if he opened it?'

'No, I don't think so,' replied Jane, 'But I couldn't be sure. Knitting patterns? Oh, I hope this doesn't mean trouble. I'll put on the kettle.'

* * * *

Jane and Katy were in the kitchen when they heard the doorbell. Katy answered it and found the brown envelope messenger standing on the doorstep again.

'What's the meaning of this?' he asked, 'It is not what I came for.'

'Oh,' responded Katy, 'Didn't Mrs Walters want the patterns?'

'I was not here to collect knitting patterns,' snapped the messenger, 'I was told to collect a document about a property.'

'Oh, that,' said Katy, 'I posted that off to Mr Walters at least two weeks ago. The UK mailing system would seem very slow.'

The visitor made no comment but turned on his heel and strode towards his car. He opened the passenger door and got in. Katy tried to see who the driver was, but without success.

She closed the door and turned around to find Jane standing in the hall.

'I don't like the sound of that,' she said, but before she could say anything else, the phone rang.

'Would you get that Jane, please?' asked Katy, 'Nature's calling.'

Jane lifted the receiver and said, 'Hello.'

'Mrs Walters?' came the query, 'Jack Caley again.'

'Hello, Jack,' said Jane. 'And what can I do for you this time?'

'I'm fairly sure that the person found dead in the Manchester apartment was your husband. I'm sorry.'

'James has been dead to me for years,' responded Jane, 'So what happens now?'

'I'm not going to ask you to come and identify him; he's not a pretty sight,' said Jack, 'The fingerprints will prove it one way or another. My Sergeant, Lesley Connor, is flying over to the Isle of Man tomorrow,' Jack continued, 'Could you meet her and fix her up with digs? She is going over to speak with you and Katy specifically.'

'I will do that, and I'm sure Katy will allow her to stay here.' After a brief hesitation, Jane asked, 'Would it be against regulations to keep me informed about your findings?'

'It may be against regulations, but I will make a point of keeping you updated,' answered Jack.

Jane then told Jack about their visitor and the knitting patterns, which made him laugh. She also mentioned the second, rather threatening, visit.

'Interesting,' commented Jack, 'I'll tell that story to Sergeant Connor, and she can have a think about what best to do. She is an excellent detective, so talk freely to her. Goodnight, Mrs Walters.'

Jack didn't mention the African connection; he would leave that to his Sergeant. Without consulting his superiors, Jack called into Lesley's office and told her to make arrangements for the trip to the Isle of Man the following day.

'Find out what the women know about the other English director, David Kingston. I'll continue to look into things at this end, and we can confer on your return.'

Chapter 24 - Intrigues

David Kingston was not a happy man. James Walters had left him to close the Scottish office, delete any references to Equinox, and to make sure there were no loose ends. On the answer machine Kingston found several calls most of them from Walters' contact in Lagos but three from Victor Oluwaseyi. The last message caused Kingston's stomach to tighten in fear.

Oluwaseyi had discovered that his name had been forged and that Walters and Adebayo had emptied and closed the African company bank account. The message closed with 'look over your shoulders, you, Adebayo and your other Isle of Man directors.' Yes, keep looking over their shoulders.

Walters had assured Kingston that all their profits were safe in separate Cayman accounts; they were under their fictitious names, and virtually untraceable. Kingston had committed his name 'King' and his account number to memory.

He had then decided to contact Walters and suggest they both disappear and set up homes in the Cayman Islands. Kingston phoned Walters in Manchester, but his call went to voicemail, so he left a message saying that he was on his way to visit.

* * * *

The Scottish business now complete, David Kingston flew to Manchester. He called at James' apartment building but hid in the toilet when a plainclothes policeman, whose face he thought was familiar, entered the building, accompanied by a Constable. He emerged from the toilet, keeping in the shadows until they entered the lift. Then he questioned one of the tenants who had just come through the front door as to why the police were here.

'There was a suspicious death in one of the apartments a few nights ago,' he told David, 'The place has been swarming with police ever since.'

David asked, 'Which apartment? I have a friend living here.'

'Sorry, I don't know. It's one of the upstairs ones. I live on the ground floor,' the tenant replied.

Another person, an elderly lady, entered the apartment building and headed for the lift. David joined her and, as they ascended, asked about the excitement a few nights ago.

'Oh, yes,' she said, 'It was on the floor below me. We were out of our apartments for ages and then imprisoned for the rest of the evening and night. My friends who live on the floor where the police were working told me they were there all night and are still coming and going.'

'Well, well!' remarked David as the lift stopped and she alighted, 'Much excitement.'

She answered him, but by then the doors were closing, and he missed her comment.

As the lift descended, it stopped at the next floor, and a gentleman entered.

'Some excitement on your landing the other night, I hear,' said David.

'Yes, a suspicious death in apartment number four,' the travelling companion replied, 'I didn't know the occupant—he was seldom there—but I think his name was Walters.'

The lift stopped, and they both alighted on the ground floor.

'Well, good-day,' said David. He waited till the other occupants left before leaving himself. Now he was more than worried; he was frightened. Could the dead man in apartment four be James? If so, what would be his next move? Perhaps Victor had the right idea, and he would also need to get lost. But where would he go?

What about Katy? Had she posted the sales notice? If so, was it now in the hands of the police? Would they realise its significance? There were too many questions and not enough answers. His mind continued to overflow with questions. Should he go back to the Isle of Man?

He had travelled there following the African trip and had taken a flat in Douglas. It was from there that he had visited Kingsway Mansion, confronted another intruder, questioned him, got into a struggle with him and—completely unplanned and unfortunately—killed him. He wondered if this man had also been looking for the document? He never said anything, just tried to run until Kingston's knife stopped him. He hadn't meant to kill the man, only threaten him but when he struggled the knife had gone straight in. Kingston shuddered at the memory; he was packing to leave the island when James had contacted him about Scotland. They arranged to meet at the Glasgow Courtyard Hotel and stay over-night there before travelling to the office on the Isle of Mull. They had purchased an empty building there, where they kept all the Great Britain records. Times had been good, and they'd managed to sell off land to gullible clients for big profits. They had covered their tracks well, except for the Ayre project on the Isle of Man. They should never have trusted Joel, and now his sister could cause problems. James had been foolish to let her go on a promise. He knew he couldn't let the matter drop; he would have to find out where the sales document was and destroy it.

The following day, David Kingston phoned the police station for information about the death in James' apartment block but became suspicious when the desk Sergeant became evasive and asked too many questions. Kingston checked out of his Manchester hotel and, sure that no one could connect him to the dead man in Kingsway, booked a flight to the Isle of Man. On his way to the airport, he removed the phone SIM card and threw the phone into a street bin.

※ ※ ※ ※

'Sir,' said Sergeant Connor, calling from Ronaldsway Airport, 'I had a text from Nick, my contact in Africa. The police have arrested one of the African directors of that Equinox company.'

'That's good news,' responded DCI Caley, 'And SOCO has been in touch, too. The fingerprints from the camera match those taken from the corpse and the apartment. James Walters is our cadaver.'

'Enjoy your stay on the Isle of Man,' Jack continued, 'Ask Mrs Walters or Katy to show you the island sights. Remember, all work and no play, and so forth.'

He disconnected with Connor and then called his mother.

'Is this a social call?' she asked.

He said it was and told her they were planning to make it to the Isle of Man before the end of August.

'If we arrive on the twenty-second, I'll have a chance to see the motorbike races.'

'Excellent! I will mark the date on my calendar. Make sure to tell my lovely grandsons that there are just fourteen more sleeps until their visit.'

When the called ended, she thought to herself, 'I don't see enough of my family, especially those lovely grandsons, Raymond and Brian.'

More computer results from SOCO showed that, apart from Walters, there was no match for any of the other fingerprints found in the apartment.

Sergeant Wilkes appeared again: 'I have just had a call from a Mr King asking to speak to the officer in charge of the investigation into the death in the Barlow Moor Road apartment. He said he had a friend living there and hasn't been able to get in touch with him. I told him you weren't available and asked for the name of his friend and for a contact number. He ended the call, but I checked, and it was a mobile. I rang the number but got no response.'

'Right, thanks,' said the DCI, 'Try the mobile operators and see if they can help.'

Sometime later, as Jack was putting things away for the evening, the redoubtable Sergeant Wilkes again knocked on his door.

'The phone company was very helpful, and I requested a record of all calls made to and from that mobile. I asked them to send the info to you, sir.'

'Good work, Wilkes,' said Jack, 'I'm off now. I am going back to the apartment block. The manager is showing me CCTV recordings from the camera in the lobby.'

'Righto, sir. Good evening,' said Sergeant Wilkes and returned to man his desk.

* * * *

The manager of the apartment blocks greeted DCI Caley in the lobby, 'Good evening, Inspector. The office is this way.'

Before following him, Jack asked, 'Where is the CCTV camera?'

'Ah, because we had had some unsavoury characters enter the building, usually waiting for someone to exit, and then slipping in before the door closed, I had a hidden camera installed. If you look closely, you will see it behind the artificial flowers on the wall facing the entrance.'

Jack looked up and eventually saw the camera cleverly disguised between the flowers.

'Excellent,' he said and followed the manager to his office.

'These are the discs for the last two weeks,' he told Jack, 'I usually only keep the recordings for ten days before reusing them, but because of the recent incident, I decided to hold on to them. I had a feeling you might want to see them.'

'Thank you, sir,' said Jack, 'That was good thinking; I should have had the sense to ask earlier.' Jack invited the manager to join him for an evening meal.

'You can help with picking out strangers,' he suggested

The manager whose name was Ralph Woodstock called his assistant and explained what was happening. Jack took the discs and he and Ralph left the building.

Jack drove back to his home, where Laura greeted Ralph warmly. Jack looked in on the boys and told them about the trip to the Isle of Man. They were very excited at the prospect, and so was he.

Laura poked her head round the door: 'And so am I,' she said, 'Now, dinner is ready.'

Following their meal, the boys tidied up and placed the dishes in the dishwasher; it was their contribution to the daily chores. Jack asked Laura to look at the discs along with him and Ralph. She produced her laptop and, one by one, they scoured the discs. The manager pointed out the folk coming and going who were residents and some whom he knew to be visitors. He recognised none who were strangers and there were quite a few.

'Any of those could be our killer,' said Jack. Suddenly, Jack found an image that interested him. They both watched as a man entered the lobby and stood in the shadow of the ornamental plant. He then approached and talked with another man.

'Pity we haven't sound,' said Jack.

'Hold it there,' said Laura, pausing the video. 'I have an idea. I'll be back in a few minutes.'

Jack's eyes followed her as she left the house. Puzzled, he rose and put on the kettle to make a pot of coffee. He had just brought it to the table when Laura returned, accompanied by a neighbour, Willie Loughry, from two doors away.

'Willie will hopefully provide your sound,' Laura announced.

'Laura has asked me to lip read,' explained Willie, 'I work with deaf children and adults. My mother was deaf, so my family and I learned sign language and lip reading from an early age.'

'Right,' said Jack, 'Have a look at this, please.'

He replayed the disc, and Willie watched as the conversation between the two men took place.

'Okay,' said Willie, and Jack expectantly paused the recording, 'One man is asking why the police are there. The other man's lips I can't see. The first guy asks which apartment and says he has a friend living here. That is all I can tell you.'

Jack then pushed the play button, and the recording continued. A lady came in, and the man followed her to the lift. There was no conversation before the two persons entered.

'Thanks, Willie, that was very helpful. It would appear our man's friend was probably the one who lived in apartment four.'

The four sat and had coffee, and Jack explained that he was the investigating officer regarding a suspicious death. As Willie rose to leave, Laura thanked him once again for his help and walked with him to the door.

'I have a suspicion you know who our mystery man is,' said Laura on her return.

'Yes,' replied Jack, 'I'm fairly sure he is a guy named David Kingston. I know him from when I lived on the Isle of Man. Can you copy his picture from the disc, Laura?'

'Of course, no problem,' she replied, and proceeded to do just that; she opened her picture gallery, and there was the photo.

'You are going to have to get more computer literate,' she teased him.

'Why should I,' laughed Jack, 'When I have someone as beautiful and intelligent as you to help me?'

'Do you want this photo printed?' asked Laura, after kissing her husband.

'Yes,' responded Jack, 'And could you email it to Sergeant Connor?'

Jack showed Laura the email address on his phone, and in seconds, the picture was on its way.

Jack then thanked Ralph and drove him back to the apartment block.

Later that evening Jack called Connor and brought her up to date on the investigation.

'Show the photo to Katy and Mrs Walters,' he said, 'And ask if they know the man.'

'I'll do that. I'll show it to them tomorrow. I have heard some interesting stories about Africa and the adventures of Mrs Walters' son, Simon. And I am meeting with Detective Lewis tomorrow afternoon. I'll let you know how I get on, and if nothing else transpires here, I'll come back on Thursday.'

Jack slept well, considering all the things that were going through his mind. He kissed Laura goodbye early next morning, then called into the apartment block and gave the manager back the tapes, save the one with, hopefully, David Kingston's photo. Later, at the office, he downloaded the messages from David Kingston's phone and printed them. The last call was from the Isle of Man. He left the office and asked Wilkes to check the numbers with the phone people and see if they could provide names for some of them.

After fruitless attempts to trace the names using the mobile numbers including Kingston's, Ken Wilkes phoned another number.

'Hello, Joe,' he said, 'It's Ken Wilkes here – Sergeant Ken Wilkes, that is.'

'Well, well!' came the answer, 'Long time, no hear.'

'Joe, I need a favour,' said Ken, 'Could we meet for coffee?'

'This sounds ominous but intriguing,' came the reply, 'When and where?'

'Geordies, at eleven?' asked Ken.

'Geordies at eleven it is, then,' responded Joe.

As Sergeant Wilkes replaced the receiver, his mind went back to when he first met Joe. Although he'd started his career as a Constable at the Salford police station, Ken had spent some time with the Met in London. He had never sought a promotion; he was more of a 'Dixon of Dock Green' type of policeman. His wife had been a police officer, too. After her death, in the line of duty, Ken had put in for a transfer back to Manchester. She was a Salford girl originally, and he wanted to bury her ashes there.

His connection with Joe came about when the so-called distribution of wealth plan, conjured up by Andrew Ferguson and Frank Smith (whose real name was Frank Singleton), turned out to be a money-laundering scheme. The fall came about when Andrew got greedy and tried to handle some of the schemes on his own. Subsequently, the fraud squad, with whom Constable Ken Wilkes worked, caught up with the cheats, and conviction and jail followed. Ferguson and Singleton each received six years, but Joe, because he was the operator, was jailed for ten. During the various interviews leading up to the arrests and trial, Ken had got to know Joe well and unsuccessfully tried, through his superiors, to have Joe's sentence reduced. He had visited Joe in prison and stood up for him at his appeal. The court eventually reduced Joe's sentence to five years.

Sergeant Wilkes organised time out with his superior officer and changed into his civvies. He left the station and headed for Geordies.

Chapter 25 – Joe

Freddy Erskine was smart at school and wanted to go to university, but times were hard in Glasgow in the fifties, so he became an apprentice joiner with a local firm of cabinet-makers. He and his wife, Marie, moved from Glasgow to Manchester in 1967, when Joe was just a baby. A joiner by trade, Freddy found there was plenty of work available in Manchester. They lived in Cheetham Hill, where Joe's two sisters were born, and Freddy found a settled job with a local building firm. Joe grew up in an area where the poverty of the sixties was still evident; his schoolmates were often involved in petty crime. Joe was never inclined to get involved in such activities. He was ignored by most of his school-mates or scoffed at for being a swot.

In his teens, he joined an evening class at the technical college to learn about the new computer languages and what was known as Information Technology. His tutor soon discovered that Joe had a talent for IT and persuaded him to leave school and to work with him as a computer technician. Joe loved his work; in his twenties, he found a job with a computer company in Salford.

When his father died from a heart attack in 1984, Joe became the primary breadwinner. His two sisters, Winnie and Grace, left school to work in a local bakery. Their three wages managed to help pay the mortgage on the house, and their mum took in washing and ironing to bolster the income.

Winnie married when she was eighteen, and the wedding costs were almost crippling. It was then that Guy Williams, a director with the computer firm, approached Joe with a proposition.

'Joe,' he said, 'A customer of mine needs the help of someone with your experience. I've arranged for you to meet with him in my office at three o'clock today; I know he will make it worth your while.'

At a few minutes to three o'clock, Joe knocked on the director's office door.

'Come in, Joe,' came the reply.

He entered to find the company director, Andrew Ferguson, seated behind his desk. There was no one else in the room.

'Take a seat, Joe,' he said, 'My friend will arrive shortly; before he comes, however, I want you to have this.' And he shoved an envelope across the desk. Joe opened it and found that it contained a rather substantial sum of money.

'That is a cash bonus for the work you have been doing,' he said, and added, 'And for what I know you will do for my friend.'

Joe removed the cash from the envelope – a hundred pounds!

'This is very generous, sir,' said Joe, 'Thank you.' He couldn't help thinking to himself how useful such a sum would be under the present household circumstances.

There was a knock at the door, and as Mr Ferguson rose to open it, Joe pocketed the envelope of money.

'Come in, Frank,' invited the director, 'This is Joe, one of my most trusted employees. Joe, meet Frank Smith, my friend and colleague.'

Joe rose and shook Frank's outstretched hand, 'Pleased to meet you, Mr Smith,' he said.

'Just Frank, please,' came the reply, 'And thank you for meeting with me.'

Joe inwardly smiled to himself and thought, 'I didn't have much choice.'

'Now then, Frank,' said Ferguson, 'Explain to Joe what it is you need. He has been a great help to our finance department over the last few weeks.'

'Well, it's like this, Joe: I want to give my family members some gifts, and let me assure you, it is not as if I am trying to defraud the tax people. But I haven't declared the cash that I have; it's not in the bank, you see, but it is a tidy sum, and I don't want it on my premises. So, I want to distribute it to my sons and daughters. I am going to recommend they put their shares into savings. This way, Mr Taxman will get his portion. As for me, I have been saving this cash, well, for some years, and to declare it now – well, I just feel it would be complicated.'

'Why not just give them the cash?' asked Joe.

'Ah, well, that, too, is complicated,' said Frank, 'I have three wives and children with each of them, and if their mothers learn of it, they will come knocking on my door. You see, being bankrupt, they think I'm broke.'

'Oh, I see,' said Joe, although alarm bells started ringing in his head. Smith – money laundering – trouble!

Mr Ferguson then butted in: 'Look, Joe, your name will not come up in this deal. I'm confident, though, that you can keep my friend out of trouble.'

'Joe, you will partake of a portion of my gifts, as a thank you,' said Mr Smith.

Somehow, Joe knew that the whole business stank, but he decided to play along.

'Okay,' he said, 'How much is involved?'

'Three million pounds,' said Smith.

Joe's mouth dropped open, 'That's a lot of money.'

'I know,' Smith responded, 'But will you help me?'

'Can I think about it?' Joe asked.

'I don't have a lot of time,' said Smith, 'You see, what I didn't tell you is that I have an incurable disease and only a few months to live.'

'Okay,' said Joe, 'Give me until tomorrow.'

'Thank you, Joe,' Frank said, 'Tell Andrew your decision, and I will see you at my office when you have figured out your plan; that is if you agree to help.'

'Joe,' said Mr Ferguson, 'Why don't you take the rest of the day off? Have a good think and come and see me in the morning.'

'Thanks,' said Joe. He rose to leave: 'Goodbye, Mr Smith, and sorry to hear about your condition.'

Joe cleared his desk, avoided the questions from his colleagues and headed for his favourite café – Geordies.

* * * *

As Sergeant Wilkes entered Geordies Café he recognised Joe and sat down at his table.

'Good to see you again, Joe.'

'So, it's Sergeant Wilkes now,' greeted Joe.

They shook hands and ordered coffee and cake.

'Quite like old times,' said Joe, 'How the years have flown.'

'We've both travelled a bit since last we met,' responded Ken, 'But as you can see, I checked up on you when I came back to Manchester.'

'What can I do for you?' asked Joe, 'You don't need money laundered, I hope?' He laughed.

Ken made no comment but outlined his request to Joe: 'My DCI is involved in a murder inquiry, and he needs to find out the recipients of some mobile phone calls. Our technical department was only partially successful, failing to discover what I believe to be the most important recipients. I wondered, if I gave you the list, could you oblige me?'

He gave the list of numbers to Joe, who responded, 'My friend, I not only could, but I would. Leave the list with me, and I will be in touch.'

After coffee and a chat, they shook hands, and Joe left the café first. Ken waited a short while before he, too, headed out and walked back to the station.

Chapter 26 – Identification

At breakfast, Sergeant Lesley Connor showed the photo to Katy.

'It is David Kingston,' confirmed Katy, followed by an angry comment: 'The rat who caused Joel's death.'

Jane looked at the photo and said with surprise, 'He looks very much like a man I was behind in the queue at Sainsbury's in Douglas yesterday.'

Just then, Lesley's mobile rang. It was DCI Caley.

'Connor, any identification on the photo?' he asked.

'Yes. It is a man Katy knows. His name is Kingston, and sir,' Connor went on, 'Mrs Walters thinks she saw him in a supermarket yesterday.'

'That is possible,' said Caley, 'The last number dialled on his mobile was from the Isle of Man. Pass that info on to DI Lewis.'

'And, sir,' continued Connor, 'I believe there is another player in the game, and I don't think it is anyone connected with our dead man.'

'Yes,' said Jack, 'I agree. I might just take time out to visit my mother. I'll meet up with you there. I will talk to DI Lewis and get permission to stick my nose in.'

DI Lewis was quite agreeable to Jack getting involved and arranged to meet him at the airport.

The following morning, after apologising to Laura, and phoning his mum, DCI Caley left for the Isle of Man.

DI John Lewis himself was there to meet him, holding Jack's name up on a sign card. They exchanged greetings, and Lewis told him what Connor had updated him with. He remarked upon the possible sighting of Kingston in the Sainsbury's supermarket in Douglas too and informed Jack that Sainsbury's supermarket had CCTV installed. They decided to go there immediately.

At Sainsbury's, they contacted the manager and, after showing their identification, asked to see Wednesday afternoon's CCTV discs.

They followed the manager to his office, where he opened a cupboard and produced a box of discs.

He looked through them, then said, 'Ah, here we are. The Wednesday afternoon recording.' He handed it to DI Lewis.

The men left and headed for Kingsway Mansion. Mrs Walters met and welcomed the two police officers.

'Hello, Chief Inspector Lewis,' she said, when Jack introduced him, 'And welcome home, Jack Caley.'

To Lewis' amazement, she gave him a hug.

'I knew him when he was a boy,' Jane explained.

Inside the house, Katy and Sergeant Connor met them, and Katy ushered them into the living room.

'Sergeant Connor,' asked Lewis, 'Have we met before?'

'I thought your name was familiar when I heard it,' she answered, 'And now, with a face to go with it – yes. We met at a conference in Manchester. I remember because we had both just received our Sergeant stripes.'

'Ah, yes,' Lewis replied. 'We were a bit younger then.'

DCI Caley interrupted their reminiscence: 'We would like to use your DVD player please, Katy.'

'Help yourself,' she responded and handed Jack the remote control.

Mrs Walters suggested she make refreshments, but Jack asked her to stay for the viewing.

On the TV, the shoppers appeared. Jack fast-forwarded the pictures until Mrs Walters' face appeared on the screen. He slowed the player down, and all four watched until both Katy and Jane shouted in unison, 'There he is!'

DCI Caley pressed the pause button, and there, on the screen, was the face of Mr David Kingston. Now Jack had a face to go with the name.

Mrs Walters said, 'Now, I'll go and make drinks. What will it be? Tea or coffee?'

All asked for coffee, and Jane left the room.

'Katy,' said Jack, 'Tell me all you know about David Kingston.'

As they all drank their coffee and ate Jane's short-bread biscuits, Katy related their association with Kingston. She started on the Isle of Man and his links with Joel, then moved on to Africa and the business of the camera and finally the kidnapping in Scotland and her involvement with James Walters.

Following the lengthy narrative, most of which some of the listeners knew already, DI Lewis asked about the messenger who called for the document. Once again, Katy, with Jane's help, painted a picture of a threatening character who mentioned a displeased employer.

'And you haven't heard from him since?' asked Lewis.

'No,' replied Kate, 'But we have had friends working in the stables, and that may have been a deterrent to anyone calling around.'

'When he handled your bogus envelope, was he wearing gloves?' Connor asked.

'Good thinking, Sergeant,' Jack remarked.

'I'll get it,' volunteered Katy.

'I'll go with you,' said Sergeant Connor, 'And I will need a plastic bag.'

They returned with the envelope securely bagged.

'Right,' said Jack, 'I think we'll leave you. Connor, maybe you could stay for another day or two, just in case our mystery visitor calls again.'

Taking the bagged envelope, the two detectives left, and Jane went to the kitchen to prepare lunch. Connor washed up the coffee cups, then went to her room to put her thoughts down on paper. Katy decided to work in the stables.

After lunch, she and Jane needed to go shopping and invited Connor to join them. The Sergeant, however, chose to stay.

'Just in case you have visitors,' she said, 'I have a sort of . . . premonition.'

'Ooh,' said Jane, 'One of those?'

'No, not a psychic,' laughed Connor, 'But sometimes we Sergeants get gut feelings. Enjoy your afternoon, ladies.'

Jane gave her mobile number to Lesley. 'Call me,' she said with a laugh, 'Just in case your 'gut feeling' becomes a reality.'

* * * *

Connor brought her paperwork to the kitchen, made a cup of coffee, and sat down to complete her notes. She was there for about an hour and had started dozing when the noise of a car on the gravel drive roused her.

'Goodness, are the ladies back already?' she asked herself.

Connor looked out the kitchen window; it wasn't their car. She noted down the number and watched as the car door opened and the man that Jane and Katy had described stepped out. She grabbed her mobile and dialled her DCI. When Jack answered, she told him what was happening and that, if they weren't too far away, she would try and keep the guy occupied.

'Unfortunately, we are in Douglas,' replied Jack, 'But DI Lewis will contact Ramsey police. Connor, be careful.'

She answered the doorbell and saw the surprised look on the man's face.

'Oh, I was expecting Miss Galloway,' he said.

'She and Mrs Walters are in the stables, I think,' said Connor, 'Shall I show you?'

'Thank you,' he replied, 'And you are?'

'Just a guest, staying till Friday. How do you know Katy?' Connor asked as they walked to the stables.

'Just a business acquaintance,' he replied.

The stables were empty when they arrived, so Connor apologised and offered him a coffee if he would like to wait: 'I'm sure they won't be long. Katy was keen to complete her work in the stables today; I know that.'

'Thank you, but I will call again,' he said, 'No rush.'

'Perhaps I could persuade you to stay,' said Connor, producing her police identification, 'I believe you can help us with our inquiries.'

'I don't think so,' the man replied, and he sprinted towards the car.

Just as a police car entered the driveway, the messenger's driver started his engine and sped away, crossing the grass to avoid the oncoming vehicle. The messenger stopped in his tracks and turned to face Connor. He pulled a gun from his pocket.

'I wouldn't try anything, sir,' she said.

The door of the police car opened, and two policemen emerged from their vehicle.

One shouted, 'Now then, Mr Whoever-You-Are, don't do anything stupid. You don't want the murder of a police officer on your record, do you?'

The man hesitated and said, 'Look, I am only a messenger, and the gun's empty.' He bowed his head in defeat as he dropped the weapon.

'Let's go inside,' said Connor, displaying her ID to the two policemen, 'As I said, I believe you can help with our inquiries.'

Sergeant Connor called Jane's mobile and explained what had happened. Five minutes later, Jane and Katy arrived.

The policemen waited until DCI Caley and CI Lewis arrived.

'I'll broadcast the car number throughout the island and see if we can trace it,' one of them, Constable Jeffers, said, taking his leave.

Mr Messenger refused to give any information following his arrest and caution. He used the well-worn phrase *'no comment'* to respond to every question Connor asked.

'You owe no loyalty to your driver friend; he left you in the lurch,' she tried.

He only looked at her bleakly and said nothing.

'Right,' said Lewis, 'I'll take him to the station.'

He was led away in handcuffs.

Lewis nodded to Caley and Connor, 'I'll let you know of any developments,' he said and followed the policemen to their car.

A moment later, Lewis returned. Addressing Lesley and Jack, he said, 'I just heard that Kingston is under arrest; they got him at the airport this morning. The man hasn't a clue about covering his tracks. You two had better come with me; he will be yours to interview.'

'You go with DI Lewis, sir,' said Connor, 'I'll join you later. I want to make sure the ladies are happy enough staying on their own.'

When Connor broached the subject to Jane and Katy, Katy laughed.

'We are very sure, especially after what happened this morning; we will have no sinister visitors. You have a murder to solve, Sergeant. Off you go!'

Suddenly, Sergeant Lesley Connor had another of those gut feelings. But this time it wasn't about the ladies – it was about the situation in Manchester.

'I think, as long as you're sure, I'll pack and prepare to return to England,' said Connor.

'We're sure. Go and pack,' replied Jane with a smile.

'I'll drive you to the police station,' Katy offered.

'Thanks,' Lesley replied, 'And thanks for your hospitality.'

'Why not come back again when our bed and breakfast business is up and running?' Jane suggested.

'I might do that,' Lesley responded.

With her bags packed, she was ready to go; she and Katy left Kingsway Mansion and walked to the car.

Meanwhile, Jane rang Simon, and they had a long chat. With quite a few 'wows' from Simon, Jane brought him up to date on the island's events. She then learned from Simon that a few folks had looked at the apartment, and the agent felt that a sale was imminent. This was good news to Jane, as she wanted to put her share of the B&B costs into the account she and Katy had set up.

Simon then told her about his visits to Kinross and his meetings with the young church's proposed elders and leadership team. The church building was an old warehouse on the outskirts of the town, but already well equipped with a kitchen and toilets, although some renovations would be required to satisfy the health and safety codes. The building was over two floors, and plans were well underway to convert the downstairs into a worship centre with various rooms for offices, prayer and Bible study. The upstairs would provide rooms for the Sunday school and crèche, and an extended portion would make an ideal games room. As soon as the plans were approved—and they were very confident they would be—work on the building would begin. Simon, meanwhile, had acquired accommodation in Kinross, and the church had arranged to begin meetings in the local secondary school in September. The principal and caretaker were both Christians; indeed, the principal was prepared to be one of the new church elders.

Jane smiled at Simon's excited narrative and agreed that, when September came, she would visit. Simon thought that perhaps he could squeeze in a visit to the Isle of Man before the end of August.

'That would be great,' said his mum, 'And Katy would be delighted to see you.'

At the mention of Katy, Simon felt his heart beat faster. He wondered if Joel's throw-away remark had something of a prediction about it.

Chapter 27 - Kingston

Kingston was a frightened man.

'What to do? Where to go?' he asked himself, 'I think I would be safer in Africa.' There was nothing left for him here, or in the UK. He could lose himself in South Africa; he knew a few folks in Johannesburg, and the police from Lagos would surely not dare to look for him there.

The following morning, Kingston packed and, at eight o'clock, phoned the airport. He also called another number; the answer made him smile.

His stomach butterflies were suddenly gone now freedom was just around the corner – well, three flights away.

Two police officers approached him as soon as he entered the terminal at Ronaldsway, and his butterflies returned. His nerves were not brought on by the men approaching him, however, but by the face of the man standing not far behind them. The oncoming officers stopped in front of him and produced their warrant cards.

'Police,' one said, 'Mr David Kingston?'

'No,' Kingston replied, 'My name is Walters. Why do you ask?'

The policemen produced a picture: 'The man in this photo looks just like you, and his name is David

Kingston. We would like you to accompany us to the police station, Mr Kingston.'

One took his case, the other his arm, and David Kingston was walked without fuss to the waiting police car.

At the police headquarters, DCI Caley conducted the interview with David Kingston, with DI Lewis present.

A short while into the interview the desk Sergeant knocked and entered with a phone in his hand, 'A call for your prisoner, it's his solicitor.'

Lewis nodded, and the Sergeant passed the phone to a puzzled Kingston. Lewis intercepted it and switched the handset to speaker.

Kingston took the phone and said, 'Hello, David Kingston'

'David,' said the caller, 'It's John Myston, your advocate. My wife, Mary, saw your arrest at the airport; I thought I would have heard from you.'

'No,' responded Kingston, 'It's a misunderstanding. I'll let you know if I need you.'

As he ended the call, Sergeant Connor joined DI Lewis and DCI Caley in the interview room. The three interrogated Kingston for an hour, each putting questions to him. His answers were vague regarding himself, and unhelpful, especially with respect to the death of James Walters. He knew nothing about the man who'd visited Katy and Jane.

Not long into the interview, DCI Caley had the feeling that Kingston seemed resigned to his fate, even relieved. Indeed, both detectives were rather puzzled by his attitude. Caley suspended the interview and paused the tape; the three police officers left the room, leaving a Constable with Kingston.

Over coffee, DCI Caley, DI Lewis and Sergeant Connor discussed the prisoner's attitude.

'He hasn't asked for his advocate,' remarked Lewis, 'Which is most unusual, as it's usually the first request.'

'He looks relieved to be in custody,' Connor remarked.

'You know,' said Jack, with a laugh, 'I think you have hit the nail on the head.'

Meanwhile, with a smile playing about his lips, Kingston, recalling the man he had noticed at the airport, thought to himself, 'Little do they know, but I feel safer in here than out there.'

When the detectives returned, DCI Caley switched on the tape and resumed the interview.

He began, 'I am a little confused by your attitude, Mr Kingston.'

Before he could continue, Kingston interrupted, 'Have you found out yet whose body was in the Manchester apartment?'

'Hold on,' interjected DI Lewis, 'DCI Caley is asking the questions here.'

'I'm saying nothing more till you answer me.' Looking at Caley, he repeated his question.

'The investigation is still ongoing,' replied Jack, 'But we suspect the dead man was your partner in crime, James Walters. Have you any idea who might have killed him, or why?'

Kingston then told them of the fraudulent property deals in Africa and in the UK.

'Some of our deals cost certain people a lot of money; maybe someone caught up with him,' replied David.

'We need a list of those clients, in the UK and any clients here on the Isle of Man,' said Connor. Then her mobile beeped, so she excused herself.

'There is one only client with connections to the Isle of Man,' David Kingston replied, 'You should know about him – that is if you have seen the relevant piece of paper.'

'I gather you mean Mr Jacob Levinson, and yes, we have the fraudulent sales document and contract,' answered Jack.

Kingston admitted to assisting Walters in Katy's kidnap but was adamant he knew nothing more about him or Africa.

'Joel and I were just small fry in the operations,' he said, 'Walters and the African directors were the big guys.'

When Sergeant Connor returned to the interview room, DCI Caley decided that he could achieve nothing else by continuing. When Lewis terminated the interview Kingston asked, 'So, what happens now?'

'You'll stay in jail here for the present,' replied Jack, 'Until we can arrange your transfer to Manchester.'

Connor fetched the custody Sergeant to take Kingston back to the holding cell.

DCI Caley wanted to talk with DI Lewis, but Connor said that Sergeant Wilkes had texted her.

'He has positive news about the list of phone calls you asked him to check,' she said, 'Apparently, our people were not entirely successful, but Sergeant Wilkes, very mysteriously, said he had help from an expert. I can do no more here so I'm going back to Manchester.'

'Good plan,' said Jack, 'I'll see you at headquarters – whenever.'

* * * *

Sergeant Wilkes met Connor at Manchester Airport, 'I'm your taxi service today. I grabbed the chance to get some time away from the station.'

'So,' asked Lesley, 'Who is your mysterious information provider?'

'His name is Joe,' replied Wilkes, 'I met him on a case of money laundering. I visited him in prison, and I think I helped in getting his sentence reduced; well, he's convinced I did. Joe is a super IT man, and he managed to find answers that evaded our IT team.'

'I'd like to meet him,' said Connor.

'Not possible, I'm afraid,' Sergeant Wilkes responded, 'His decision, not mine.'

At the police headquarters, Ken Wilkes showed his colleague the list of names that both the police team and Joe had uncovered. Lesley whistled in amazement at some of the names. By the tone of their messages, they gathered they were people whom Kingston and the company had defrauded. She noticed that Kingston's name also appeared on the list of mobiles checked. When she enquired, Wilkes told her of his call to the police station.

'Ken, could you scan the pages, and email them to DCI Caley?' Connor asked, 'He is spending tonight with his mum and returning tomorrow, but I think he would want to see the list.'

Sergeant Connor looked through the emails on the station network and found a message from the SOCO team. She read that the killer had made a mistake when leaving Walters' apartment by the fire escape by leaving a portion of plastic glove that had caught and torn on a screw head in his getaway. On it he'd left a thumbprint. The message went on to say that, unfortunately, the print matched nothing they already had on file.

Connor called DCI Caley on his mobile. When he answered, she passed on the SOCO message, and then said, 'Sir, I wonder if that fingerprint would match the man DI Lewis questioned, or perhaps something that belonged to Kingston.'

'Good thinking,' said her boss, 'I'll get on to DI Lewis. I'll also ask him to have Kingston's belongings fingerprinted; he had cryptic, unsigned notes among the stuff from his pocket. Thanks, Lesley. I'll see you tomorrow.'

Jack phoned DI Lewis and made his request.

'I'll get someone from my team on to it right away, but I was just about to phone you. A high-class English solicitor turned up a while ago and posted bail for our mysterious messenger. The solicitor asked for him by name.'

Jack could hear Lewis laughing to himself before he continued, 'His name is Karl Andrews, Karl with a K, and he is originally from—wait for it—Manchester. Your people may have him on record.'

'Thanks,' Jack answered, 'I'll see if we have anything on a Karl Andrews. Indeed, I'll ask Connor to check.'

Jack phoned and instructed Connor to check if Manchester had anything on Karl, with a K, Andrews.

Chapter 28 – The Priest

David Kingston sat in his cell, determined to be the model prisoner. He didn't plan to be there much longer, and he had not requested a solicitor; that would make them wonder, of course, but it didn't matter. Tonight would be the beginning of the end. The so-called advocate who called earlier would sort things out, 'What is it like to be insane?' he wondered.

The duty Constable, bringing Kingston his midday meal, heard him laugh out loud.

* * * *

Victor Oluwaseyi received the phone call at 9 a.m.:

'Kingston was leaving the island,' the caller said, 'I told him I would meet him in Manchester but your man on the island followed him to the airport where the police arrested him. So, what now?'

'Okay, leave it with me; I'll get back to you. But, meanwhile, there is something else I need you to do if we are to cover our tracks.'

Oluwaseyi outlined his request and said that he would liaise with their man on the Isle of Man and arrange to take care of Kingston. He rang a mobile number and asked to speak to Max. The mention of this name, of course, was a coded signal; the call was then transferred to an Isle of Man number.

During the call, Oluwaseyi discussed the situation regarding David Kingston, and a plan was put in place to dispose of their former asset. The group of fraudsters always had a plan, should one of them be arrested. It had worked with Adebayo. Hopefully, it would work with Kingston. It was time, once again, to contact the priest.

* * * *

The cell door window opened, and the duty Constable said, 'You've got a visitor.'

The cell door opened to admit the black-clad cleric.

'Mr Kingston,' the priest said, 'You sent for me. My name is Father Flanagan.'

David was surprised to discover that Father Flanagan was black.

'Don't look so surprised, David,' whispered the priest, as the cell door closed behind him, 'I'm here to hear your confession.'

David smiled.

'I'm not sure how soundproof the door is,' continued the priest, 'But this is what happens. It succeeded with Adebayo, who, by the way, is no longer in prison, so we are sure it will also work for you. Once complete, you get a new identity, and no one will ever find you again; your reward awaits you, of course.'

'I have committed the account number to memory,' said David, 'So, what now?'

'You have to trust me,' said the priest, 'I have the injection obscured, and when I administer it, you will feel strange. After about an hour or so, you will start laughing and gibbering and slobbering from your mouth. You, of course, according to the plan, will be insane and taken from here to the hospital. The effects will wear off by the time you arrive, and everyone will be surprised. But the doctor will keep you in overnight for examination. It works every time. As for helping you escape from the hospital, well, that is a piece of cake. Are you ready?'

David nodded, and the priest bent over him. David felt the slight prick in his upper right arm and then a feeling of nausea, which passed quickly. The priest then dabbed David's shirt, the wall and the cell's window ledge with some of the contents of the syringe. He smiled to himself as he straightened up and thought how bewildered the policeman would be who next came to visit David.

He knocked on the cell door. Once it was opened, the priest turned, smiled at David and said, 'The Lord bless you and keep you, my son. Call me if you need me again.'

And with that, he made his exit.

The Constable closed the cell door, but not before he peeped in at David and mouthed a mocking, 'Hallelujah.'

David lay down on his bunk; he felt nothing for a while, and then the rigours started. He tried to call out but only choked as his throat seemed to close. His legs kicked, and with an effort, he managed to turn on his side. But then he couldn't move; the venom had taken its deadly effect. As the blackness clouded his mind he suddenly remembered that the former director who died in a Lagos prison was Adebayo.

Suddenly, he felt nothing.

David Kingston, his final journey begun, would feel nothing ever again.

Once back in his apartment, the black priest called his contact.

'The job is done; Kingston is a problem no more. Tell your boss to arrange my payment.'

* * * *

Police headquarters erupted with the news of Kingston's death. The Superintendent Harold Friel, a recent addition to the Isle of Man force, looked deathly pale as he sat with CI Lewis and the duty Sergeant, discussing the night's events. The pathologist who examined Kingston's body was convinced that he was poisoned but would know more after an autopsy and toxicology reports. The SOCO team examined the cell and found signs of liquid on Kingston's shirt and on the cell wall and windowsill. The body was then removed for the post mortem.

'The Chief Constable had me on the carpet this morning,' said Superintendent Friel. 'Get to the bottom of this and quickly' were his words. 'So, was Kingston suicidal? Or if he was poisoned, how?'

'He wasn't on suicide watch, sir,' said the Sergeant, 'Indeed, he was a cooperative and, believe it or not, contented prisoner. Talking with him, though, I felt he knew something that would be to his advantage; he had a constant smirk on his face.'

'Kingston turned out his pockets when he came in,' said DI Lewis, 'And there was nothing there unless he had a false tooth containing the poison – you know, the kind that secret agents used during the war.'

'Oh, don't be ridiculous!' screamed the Super, 'Either he had it concealed somewhere on his person, somewhere that your officers didn't find, or the culprit is one of your officers!' Then, more calmly, he asked, 'Did he have any visitors?'

'No,' replied the duty Sergeant, 'Not according to the day staff who were on duty yesterday, but the night Sergeant reported he wanted to see his priest, a Father Flanagan,' he conferred looking at his notes, 'The prisoner gave the Sergeant a phone number. The priest arrived at ten o'clock and showed identification; apparently, he was black.'

Glancing up from his notes, he asked no one in particular, 'I wonder why the duty officer found it necessary to mention that?' The Sergeant continued with his report, 'The duty Constable stood outside the cell door, and when the priest left, he examined the cell and searched Kingston – nothing suspicious was found. The priest had left only a leaflet on the Mass, which appeared innocuous.'

'Has any check been made on this black priest with the Irish name?' asked Lewis.

'Not by me,' the Sergeant responded, 'And, with all the fuss, I doubt if anyone else has. I'll phone the number and ask the priest to come in again.'

'Right,' said the Superintendent, 'What about the officer, what's his name, from Manchester, where is he?'

'He is still on the island, sir. His mother lives here. His father was a former Chief Constable,' replied John Lewis.

The Super asked, 'What is his name?'

'DCI Caley, sir.'

'Well, well, well!' responded the Super, 'Raymond Caley's son. I knew Raymond's brother, Brian, when I was an inspector. Raymond would come to the Lake District on holiday, and at times, I would go fishing with him and Brian. I never met Raymond's wife or family.'

'Chief Constable Caley had just the one son, sir, Jack. He was with the Met for a while,' tendered Lewis.

'Right. Well, we need to interrogate every officer who might have had contact with the deceased during his time in our cells and I mean *interrogate*, I don't mean just ask a question or two. Contact DCI Caley and have him come in; he might as well be a part of this fiasco. And,' he said in a voice at least an octave higher, 'Get hold of that priest!' With that, he stormed out of the office.

* * * *

At three o'clock, the Chief Constable called the Superintendent and DI Lewis to his office. A few minutes later DCI Jack Caley joined them.

'The report has come through from pathology,' the Superintendent informed them, 'David Kingston died of poisoning. The toxicology results suggest it was snake venom. Did we find a snake in the cell or anywhere on the premises?'

'No, sir,' replied Lewis.

'I'm not surprised,' continued the Chief Constable, 'The team found no sign of a snake bite. There was, however, a pinprick on his upper right arm and evidence of the same venom on the skin around the mark and on his clothing and on the cell windowsill. The pathologist suggests a dart from a blowpipe. Was any such item discovered on the body, or on his clothing?'

'It is unlikely that whoever found him, or the doctor who carried out the initial examination, would have suspected or looked for such an object,' the Superintendent remarked, 'And how on earth was the murder—because that is what it now is—carried out?'

'There is the window in the cell,' said Lewis, 'Let me go and examine the area around it; I'm not sure what's on the outside.'

'Do that,' said the Chief Constable, and with that he dismissed them.

After a fruitless investigation of the cell, DI Lewis took Jack to his office. Over coffee, they discussed the happenings of the last twenty-four hours. DCI Lewis reported that the cell window looked out on to the car park but was inaccessible from there.

The office phone rang; it was the Chief Constable.

'Lewis, the Superintendent has left for the evening, but I thought you should know the latest from the pathologist.'

Lewis put the desk phone on speaker and he and Caley listened as the Chief Constable updated them with the latest developments. The pathologist had found traces of snake venom on Kingston's shirt and his conclusion was that he had received an injection of the poison on his upper right arm.

'Sir,' said the duty Sergeant, opening the door of DI Lewis' office, 'You and the super are not going to like this. There is a priest in the Onchan parish named Flannigan and, as the name suggests, he is Irish, but he's not black. The phone number was a mobile number and not available when I tried it, and there are no black priests in any of the island parishes.'

Chapter 29 - Shot

Folks say that you never hear the shot that kills you; well, Simon did, so he knew he wasn't dead.

'Simon. Simon.'

Somewhere, in the distance, a voice was calling his name. Gradually, he opened his eyes and saw a figure in a white coat.

'Simon,' a man was saying, 'Welcome back.'

Then his mother, seated in a bedside chair, spoke his name.

'Simon, oh, Simon, I thought I had lost you.' She started crying and laughing at the same time, 'What happened? Who shot you?'

Simon could hear his mum's voice coming from what seemed like inside a drum.

'Mrs Walters,' said Doctor Lane, the man in the white coat, 'It will take time for Simon to come fully round. Best you just sit quietly and hold his hand; he will recognise you soon enough.'

Pictures whirled around and around in his head. Simon could see the church and Graham walking towards him. A sound, then pain. Blackness.

He was too exhausted to try and recall anything else.

Simon was sure he had heard his mother's voice, but she was on the Isle of Man. He heard it again, that sound, speaking his name. He struggled and, eventually, once again, opened his eyes.

'Simon.'

He turned his head towards the sound and saw the face of his mother.

'Mum,' he uttered through cracked lips, 'Where am I?'

'You are in Edinburgh Hospital,' Jane replied, 'Someone shot you!'

'How long have I been here?' he asked.

'Ten days,' was her answer, 'I've been here since Sunday evening. Graham and your friends in church sat with you at times. You got shot on Sunday afternoon; Graham says he heard the shot and saw you fall. He phoned the police and ambulance; the latter came very quickly and rushed you to hospital. Katy rings often and would like to be here but she is still involved with the police on the Isle of Man.'

Doctor Lane re-entered the ward, 'Hello, Simon. My name is Charles Lane; I'm your doctor. Mr Wade, our surgeon, operated on you and removed the bullet from the top of your spine. He is hopeful no major damage occurred; he had you put into an induced coma. You've come round much quicker than anticipated; not many patients rouse from an induced coma so fast. We have noticed signs of stirring over the last two days, and you have had a good team of watchers. The police want to speak with you, but I told them to wait. From now on, though, I will restrict the number of your visitors. Your mum, of course, can come and go as she pleases.'

Simon barely understood anything the doctor said. But one fact surged through his mind: someone wanted him dead.

Chapter 30 – Intrigue

On Friday morning Jack's office phone rang.

'DCI Caley,' Jack answered.

'Hi, sir. Lewis here. I've got some good or maybe bad news.'

'Tell me,' responded Jack.

'The priest, real name Abroon Adid, is from Mogadishu in Somalia. That's where he was born and raised but he has travelled extensively as a mercenary soldier. There are traces of his activities in several African and Asian countries. He appeared in the UK five years ago, and the Met questioned him about the death of a politician. Nothing was proved, so he was released without charge. He turned up in Scotland last year, and the police arrested him after a brawl in a nightclub. A businessman named Victor Oluwaseyi posted bail! The charges against him were subsequently dropped, and Mr Adid walked away, a free man.'

'Is that the good news or bad news?' asked Jack.

'Oh, the identification of the priest is part of the good news,' John Lewis continued, 'And he is still on the Isle of Man. The bad news is that we cannot question him. Two workmen discovered his decomposing corpse in a disused warehouse on the outskirts of Douglas. So, the murderer has been murdered, shot from close range with a pistol.'

'That sounds like the script of a James Cagney picture,' said Caley.

'Who?' asked Lewis.

'Seems I'm showing my age here,' smiled Caley in reply.

Lewis laughed, 'Only kidding! I've seen some of the old Cagney pictures. Remember the one that ended with him on top of the gasometer, shouting, 'I'm on top of the world'? Then, boom.'

'I do, indeed,' responded Jack, 'But the one I remember the most is the hitman movie where, having completed his killing, he looks for his payment—'

'And ends up with a bullet, instead,' Lewis finished.

'Yes,' said Jack, 'Just like our priest. I can picture the scenario,' he continued, 'The two arrange to meet for the payoff. The killer holds out the money with one hand, then produces a gun with the other, and, like Cagney – bang.'

'I think you've possibly cracked it, DCI Caley,' remarked Lewis, 'However, and this is the second part of the good news, I know who the killer is. It looks like he searched and removed all incriminating evidence from the victim but left a partial thumb print on his shiny belt buckle.'

'Don't tell me,' said Jack, 'Our Mr Oluwaseyi?'

'Give that man a coconut!' replied DI Lewis.

'Now,' continued the DI, 'More good news. The forensics team also discovered, hidden in a false heel in Adid's left shoe, a small USB memory stick. On it were the names of all the clients the priest killed for cash. Kingston is on the list. I'll send the contents of the stick to your computer. Let me have your contact details.'

'I'll text them to you,' said Jack, 'So, we have narrowed down our killers to two: the priest, aka Abroon Adid, and Victor Oluwaseyi. My Sergeant was in contact with a detective in Nigeria, name of Nick Lassiter, who gave her details about Oluwaseyi and others involved in the property scams.'

'Small world,' responded Lewis, 'I worked with Nick when I was a Sergeant, a long time ago now. How long has he worked in Africa?'

'He transferred, just recently, to their force,' answered Jack, 'He did work in Nigeria, and my Sergeant contacted him there; they served together at one time. Apparently, he is now working with police in Lagos. The Lagos Police Commissioner himself asked my Superintendent for Sergeant Connor's temporary assignment to work with DI Lassiter. Do you know anyone in Lagos?'

'Unfortunately, no,' DI Lewis replied. Then he laughingly added, 'Maybe I can persuade my Chief Constable to assign me to their police force.'

'Right!' said Jack, 'Maybe they'll let us both go.' He, too, laughed: 'Here's my Sergeant; I must go. Bye.' As he did he sent his email address to Lewis' mobile phone and then greeted Connor.

'Well, Sergeant?' he asked.

'It's all arranged,' replied Connor, 'I leave on Monday of next week. I'm quite excited, I must admit. I am to be involved with Nick in investigating the defunct Equinox Company and to follow up the names the Lagos police have.'

Jack's desktop computer beeped, telling him an email had arrived. He opened it, and the Isle of Man information appeared.

'Right, Sergeant. What do I do now?' he asked Connor, gesturing to the screen.

Lesley opened a drawer in the desk and took out a USB memory stick, which she inserted into the computer. She then saved the information to the device.

'There you are, sir,' said Lesley, handing the USB memory stick to Jack, 'The info is contained within.'

'I really must take a course on computing,' said Jack, as he lifted his phone receiver and dialled Superintendent Richards' extension number.

'Can Connor and I see you again, sir?' he requested, 'We need to talk about another important discovery. Right.'

Then, to the Sergeant, he said, 'We have located the priest, but I'll bring you and the Super up to speed together. Let's go.'

Superintendent office once again, DCI Caley related the information given to him by DI Lewis. After he had finished, the Superintendent sat quietly for a moment, then spoke: 'This doesn't change our plans, but I would like to see the information from the Isle of Man.'

'It's all in here, sir,' said Jack, winking to Connor. He handed the stick to the Superintendent.

'I haven't seen it yet, sir,' said Jack, 'So perhaps we could look at it together?' Then, to Connor, 'You go and put your house in order, Sergeant. Ready for your journey.'

The Superintendent made two copies of the information and handed one to Jack.

'Here you are. We can now assimilate it separately, Jack, in the privacy of our offices.'

Obviously dismissed, Jack took his copy and left. He looked at his watch and decided he could call it a day.

When he arrived home, his wife greeted him with a kiss and then said, 'Katy rang a few minutes ago. She tried your office, and someone informed her that you had left for home.'

'Yes,' said Jack, 'Katy is the girl on the Isle of Man. She is part of our inquiries.'

He rang her immediately.

'Thanks for getting back to me,' said Katy, 'I had a visitor this afternoon. A very posh-looking gentleman introduced himself as Jacob Levinson. Mr Levinson told me about the scam regarding the Ayre property. He said that perhaps the police should hear what he has to say. I think you should speak to him; he says he has an interesting story to tell. I rang to speak to DI Lewis, but he wasn't available. I would appreciate your presence when we talk again. Can you come?'

'I will,' said Jack, 'Everything is pretty well concluded here. I'll check with my Super and ring you back. Please continue to make contact with DI Lewis, though. Where is Mr Levinson now?'

'He went back to his hotel to wait on my call. I said I would contact you and phone him there,' Katy replied, 'Did you know he owned a hotel in Douglas?'

'Yes,' replied Jack. 'It came up in earlier investigations. It's named The Olympian and is located on the promenade.'

Jack disconnected with Katy, then rang his Superintendent, who was still in his office.

'Sir, Mr Jacob Levinson has surfaced. He is the gentleman involved in the Isle of Man con. I would like to go there and speak to him.'

'Yes, do that,' said the Super, 'Have you read your list yet?'

'Not yet, sir,' replied Jack.

'Get to it; it makes interesting reading. Keep me posted on developments.'

'I will, sir,' said Jack, 'Goodnight.'

After dinner, Jack booked a ferry from Heysham for 2.30 p.m. the following day. Laura decided to accompany him and bring the boys to see their grandmother. Jack read through the printed list and some of the names surprised him. One was a high-ranking police officer in Glasgow, others he recognised as important figures in the worlds of politics and television.

At six o'clock the next evening, and with hugs exchanged, the complete Caley family sat down to dinner in Gran Canley's home.

* * * *

Next morning, at five minutes past eleven, coffee arrived at a table in the lounge of the Olympian Hotel, around which sat DCI Caley, DI Lewis, Katy Galloway and Jacob Levinson.

'Gentlemen and lady,' Jacob began, 'I would have been in touch sooner, but business in New York kept me occupied for the last few weeks. I arrived on the Isle of Man yesterday and read of the death of David Kingston; I gather he was murdered.'

'He was, and by a person who himself is now dead – or, I should say, murdered,' said DI Lewis.

'Well, not by anyone in my employ, I assure you,' Jacob responded to what sounded like an implication of guilt, 'Although, as I told Miss Galloway yesterday, the threatening visitor to her home on one or two occasions was an agent of mine, Karl Andrews. I had asked him to request the sales document, but he overstepped his remit. Unfortunately, he behaved badly and ended up in custody.'

'Indeed he did and refused to cooperate. His prints, however, were on record in Manchester,' said Lewis.

'Oh yes,' interrupted Jacob, 'He was involved in an altercation with a man who was threatening my son, Abby, but he got off with a caution. Oh, and it was Abby who was the driver that day at Kingsway Mansion. I gather he drove off and left Karl. Not only so, he left the island that same evening. I caught up with him in London when he met me off my flight.'

'How did you know about the documents?' asked DCI Caley.

'Ah!' he replied, 'That information came from Katy's brother, Joel. He wrote to me and told me about the scam. I assured him I suspected as much and asked him to get and send me the bogus documents as evidence. When nothing came, I thought maybe he had changed his mind. I wasn't too bothered until I heard that he had committed suicide—'

'It wasn't suicide,' Katy broke into the narrative, 'Kingston was responsible for Joel's death.' Tears filled her eyes as she remembered: 'I'm not sorry he's dead – Kingston, I mean. My only regret is spiritual.' Katy did not elaborate further.

Lewis handed her his handkerchief, 'I always keep one handy,' he explained.

'May I continue?' asked Jacob.

'Of course. Go on,' Jack replied.

'Did you see the documents?' Jacob asked.

'We did,' said Lewis, 'Katy found it, secretly hidden by Joel. I have a copy with me; the original is evidence.' Lewis produced the paper from his briefcase.

Jacob asked, 'I wonder: did you notice my signature on it?'

Lewis studied the paper, 'Well, blow me down; I missed that!' he said, 'It's not your correct signature.' He handed it over to Jack.

Jack shook his head in disbelief, 'Crafty and safe,' he said.

'Show me, please,' asked Katy, and she, too, saw the signature:

Jacob Livingston.

'How did we miss that?' she asked.

'Livingston, Levinson,' said Jacob, 'Close enough to miss, at a glance. But, from what Joel told me in his letter, Walters, Kingston and he were not the only ones involved. He mentioned two others, African, whose names escape me at present.'

'Victor Oluwaseyi and Awale Adebayo,' DI Lewis said.

'Yes, what became of the bogus African directors?' asked Levinson, 'I never had any contact with them.'

'Kingston and Adebayo are dead, killed by an assassin in the guise of a priest, and both in the same manner. We know that Oluwaseyi, or a henchman, killed Walters, and we are certain that Oluwaseyi killed the assassin, too, in order to tie up loose ends, I suppose.'

'Yes,' said Jacob Levinson, 'A contact in Manchester informed me of Walter's demise. I didn't know about Kingston's. Where is Oluwaseyi at present?'

'In Johannesburg,' Caley answered, 'My Sergeant, Lesley Connor, and another police officer, already based in Nigeria, are investigating his contacts in Lagos.'

Jacob nodded, then rose and said, 'Thank you for coming. Please, stay for dinner.'

Seated at the table and enjoying a scrumptious meal, they talked some more about the bogus scam. Jacob learned that Katy's friend Jane was the estranged wife of James Walters. Jacob confessed, to his shame, to entertaining the concept of owning the Plain of Ayre, but Katy assured him that no such place existed. The area's real name was the Northern Plain.

'I got carried away with their convincing sales talk of a golf club and hotel,' he said, 'It was just as I came to sign that niggles started, and on the spur of the moment, I signed *Livingston* instead of *Levinson*. Walters and Kingston didn't seem to notice. We shook hands, and I took their bank details and promised to transfer the deposit, fifty thousand pounds. They said their advocate would get in touch as soon as the money was in their account. I never made the transfer, of course, because when I returned to America, Joel's letter was waiting for me.'

Turning towards Katy, he said, 'Once again, I am truly sorry about your brother. I felt I owed him a great deal, so I opened an account in his name. I sent him the details and received his signature; we were both signatories. I would like you, Miss Galloway, to let me have your account details, so I can transfer Joel's funds to you and close his account.'

'I don't know what to say,' said Katy.

'"*I accept*" would be sufficient,' responded Jacob, 'Now, coffee?'

Chapter 31 - Progress

During visiting time on Wednesday, tears filled Jane Walters' eyes as she watched Simon struggle to walk. Doctor Lane and Mr Wade both told Jane they were confident that Simon had a strong constitution.

'Believe me,' Mr Wade said, 'It will take time, but Simon will recover. Perhaps not fully, but my estimate is eighty to ninety percent. And I stress that with the injury Simon received, that is news worth cherishing.'

Simon returned, exhausted, to his bed, where his nurse made him comfortable. The physiotherapist finished writing her notes and said to Jane, 'Your son is one determined young man. I predict he will walk by himself within two weeks.'

When Simon fell asleep, Jane kissed him on the forehead and left.

She visited Simon again the following afternoon and, upon her arrival, Simon buzzed for the nurse.

'Now my mother is here,' Simon asked, 'Could we speak to Doctor Lane and Mr Wade?'

Halfway through visiting time, Mr Wade appeared, apologised for the delay and shook Mrs Walters' hand.

'Dr Lane couldn't make it; a patient needed his attention. However, Simon made a request this morning, which I chatted over with my staff. He asked if we could arrange a transfer to the hospital on the Isle of Man.

I needed to take some things into consideration. Firstly, his speech is not as good as Dr Lane would like it to be, but it has improved. And secondly, his physiotherapist agrees that there are still weaknesses in his left arm and leg. After considering all the pros and cons, and the fact that he shared with us your commitments, our decision is a positive one. We will allow the transfer, but not until next week. I also had a chat with his church pastor, who soon realised that, for the foreseeable future, Simon will not be able to perform his church duties; he is coming in this evening to talk things over with Simon.'

Again, he shook hands with Jane, nodded to Simon, then departed.

As arranged, Graham arrived after visiting hours when Jane had not left the ward. He explained that Mr Wade had spoken with him, and the church had decided to pay Simon a full year's wages in advance to cover his period of convalescence. He raised his hand to silence Simon's protest and assured him of their prayerful support, as well.

'When the time is right, and you are once again fully fit—and that, I believe, will not be too long away—Kinross will be waiting. I believe your transfer is on and that is good, for both of you. Let us pray.'

Following his prayer, Graham assured Simon and Jane that he and the leadership would continue to visit, then he said goodbye.

'Wow!' said Simon, 'That is a generous gesture, and I'm sure it came about with prayer. What a lovely fellowship; I will miss my friends.'

Just then, another visitor came through the screen curtain. It was the police inspector who had interviewed Simon following his partial recovery.

'Mr Walters,' he said, 'I have some good news for you and your mother. On Monday afternoon, a scoundrel named Arthur Pickering, a former Marine, crashed his car on the road to Newcastle. He sustained major injuries and is unlikely to survive. In the boot of his wrecked vehicle, the police found an L85 rifle; a standard issue during the Gulf War. The Newcastle police contacted us, and the weapon was checked and found to be the one used in the attack on you. He had a mobile phone, on which were several messages.' The inspector gave a slight laugh: 'I'm sorry,' he continued, 'But the last text instructed him, and in capital letters, to delete all messages and get as far away from Scotland as possible. Mr Pickering, thankfully, disobeyed. Does the name *Victor O* mean anything to you?'

Jane gasped, 'Indeed, it does. Are you suggesting that this Victor O was responsible for having my son shot?'

Jane caught her breath and then more calmly said, 'Can I suggest you contact DI Lewis at the Isle of Man police headquarters? Victor O is Victor Oluwaseyi who features strongly in one of his murder investigations. Also, DCI Caley from the Manchester police force may still be there; he is another very interested party.'

'DCI Caley contacted me when he heard of Simon's shooting,' said the inspector, 'I did say I would keep him in the loop. We've known each other from our days at police college. Thank you, Mrs Walters, for your helpful information, and get well soon, Simon. I believe you are going to the Isle of Man shortly.'

Seeing Jane's puzzled expression, he explained, 'I talked with Simon's doctor this afternoon regarding this visit; he updated me on the transfer. Well, goodnight to you both.' The inspector exited through the curtain.

ROY PORTER

Jane kissed Simon and left for home. She found a message on her answering machine from Katy.

'Hi, Jane. I didn't want to use your mobile as I reckoned you were at the hospital. How is Simon? Is there much progress?'

Jane returned her call: 'Hello, Katy,' she said and proceeded to update her young friend with all the news.

Katy was thrilled at the prospect of Simon and Jane returning to the island. Then she updated Jane on the house conversion progress.

The following morning, Jane received a call from her estate agent with the news that a new viewer had made a firm offer on her apartment. The amount of the offer, and in cash, was more than she had hoped for, so she told the agent to accept. Jane then offered up a prayer of thanks for both Simon's progress and the apartment sale and prayed that, regarding the latter, all would go through without any hitches. She thanked God for the church families in Scotland and Ramsey, for their attentiveness, prayers and finance. Rising from her knees, Jane felt a tremendous sense of peace and well-being.

Chapter 32 – Johannesburg

'Yes. Great. Thank you, Inspector.' DI Lassiter ended his call and turned to Sergeant Connor: 'They've traced Oluwaseyi to Johannesburg,' he said, 'Traced, but not yet located. However, that's progress. From the information DI Lewis sent to me, I've managed to locate connections in three African countries where Adid operated. He used different names for his various hits, but only two of them had connections to Oluwaseyi. Both were fellow directors of the Equinox Company: Adebayo and Kingston.'

'So, what now?' asked Connor.

'We will go to Johannesburg and liaise with our colleagues there,' replied Nick, 'At least, that is their suggestion. They have no criminal record on Victor Oluwaseyi and will not act unless we can prove he is a 'clear and present danger' – their words, not mine. Sounds like shades of Tom Clancy – don't ask. Let's go and talk to the commissioner and update him on all that has transpired, both here and on the Isle of Man.'

On their way to the commissioner's office, Connor did ask, 'Who is Tom Clancy?'

'Google him,' Nick said with a laugh, as he knocked on the office door.

* * * *

The flight from Lagos to Johannesburg landed at 3.15 p.m. the following afternoon. A young lady stood in the reception area of the O. R. Tambo Airport, holding a sign with DI Lasseter's name printed on it.

As Nick and Lesley approached, she smiled and said, 'Welcome. I am Sergeant Edberg,' and they shook hands. Sergeant DeBerg escorted them to an unmarked police car drawn up outside. DeBerg introduced her driver as Police Constable Jerry Kane, 'He's from your part of the globe, but so long here now he's been institutionalised.'

Constable Kane laughed and greeted the newcomers. Then he drove off towards the City Centre.

'Tell me a bit about your city,' Nick invited, 'It looked massive from the air.'

'It is, but not as big as your London,' DeBerg informed him, 'The population is over four million, and it is a very prosperous city. It's been called Africa's economic powerhouse. And, of course, it is situated in the middle of the gold and diamond area.'

The Johannesburg Metropolitan Police Station was just a half hour's drive from the airport. On arrival, Nick and Lesley were escorted into the main building and straight to the commissioner's office. Before entering, Sergeant DeBerg informed them that new rankings now applied, and his official title was General.

DeBerg knocked and was admitted, 'General,' she said, 'Let me introduce Detective Inspector Nick Lassiter and Detective Sergeant Lesley Connor. Nick and Lesley, meet General Alfred DeBerg – my father.'

'Come in and sit,' the general invited. Putting on a stern face, he said, 'Sergeant, sort out some refreshments.' He then smiled.

When Sergeant DeBerg left to do his bidding, the general welcomed them again and said, 'My daughter, Gwynne, followed not mine, but her mother's footsteps into the police force. My wife, her mum, unfortunately, died of cancer two years ago. She was from Wales, originally; hence, my girl's Christian name. When we were both at the police academy, my wife and I met in your neck of the woods, Lesley: Manchester. It was there I also came across DCI Caley's father. I believe you worked with Jack Caley, Lesley.'

'Yes, sir, I did,' she replied, finding the informality among the ranks quite strange.

Gwynne arrived with coffee and cake. They ate and drank in silence for a while, and then, General DeBerg spoke, 'So, with Victor Oluwaseyi, what can you tell me about him that would make us interested in him? I gather from my colleague in Lagos that he is a bad lot, but I need more if I am to involve my officers.'

The stories of Equinox and murder occupied his attention for the rest of the afternoon.

'I can see now why he needs locating,' said the General, 'We have your photo-fit, and one Constable was sure he recognised him at the airport last week. He can't remember why or how, but never mind that; Gwynne, I will leave this to you. Make copies of the picture and have them circulated to other stations. From what I have heard this afternoon, our officers will help. Have the hotels checked too, please, Gwynne. Oh, and speaking of hotels, are our guests sorted?'

'Yes,' replied Gwynne, 'They are booked into the Imperial. I knew you would want them well looked after,' she added with a smile.

'Right,' said General DeBerg. He looked at the new-comers, 'That will do for today. Liaise with my Sergeant, and she will keep me informed. Have a pleasant evening.'

Following handshakes and goodbyes, Gwynne drove Nick and Lesley to the Imperial Hotel and waited while they checked in.

'The General wasn't aware, but I already had copies made and circulated them today in preparation for your arrival. I didn't do the hotels; I thought that would be too presumptuous of me, but I intend to do that tomorrow. I will pick you up at 9.30 a.m. tomorrow.'

* * * *

True to her word, Sergeant DeBerg was waiting in reception when Nick and Lesley appeared next morning.

'Good morning,' she greeted them, 'I trust you slept well.'

They both returned the greeting and the three police officers left the hotel. Within minutes, they were at police headquarters.

'The traffic thins out between nine and ten o'clock,' she volunteered, 'So it is good for city travel.'

Once inside the building, Sergeant DeBerg showed them to a desk, 'You two can work from here,' she said, 'And this is my desk.' She pointed to one nearby. 'But, before anything else, let's go for coffee and a chat.'

They sat in the canteen with a large, twelve-cup, cafetière of coffee and cups on the table. By the time they were finished drinking and organising, they had formed a plan of action.

Back at their desks, they put their project into opera-tion. Sergeant DeBerg left to instruct her team of officers, while Nick and Lesley gathered a collection of copied photo-fits. With their allotted driver, a young Constable named Sally, they headed for the city's hotels, which, although just around the airport vicinity, were numerous. They drove and traipsed most of that day without success. Back at headquarters, Gwynne and her team had a similar report.

It was the following morning when Victor Oluwaseyi surfaced. Gwynne received a call from the police in Mondeor to say that their quarry had checked into the Chandler Hotel there. A plainclothes officer followed him to a café, where he had coffee with a man dressed in business clothes. He was still there.

Gwynne called Nick and reported the sighting. They arranged to meet up at headquarters.

On her computer, Gwynne brought up a street map of Mondeor and located the hotel and café.

'My colleagues in Mondeor are watching and will keep me informed of the movements of both Oluwaseyi and the other gentleman,' she said, 'We will meet with them there.'

Just then, the phone rang. Gwynne answered it and turned to Nick and Lesley: 'There has been a development: Oluwaseyi is dead, shot in broad daylight as he crossed the town square. The businessman had already left; no one knows where he's gone.'

Frustrated she continued, 'And he wasn't followed.'

Later, in the General's office, Lesley and Nick listened as the General outlined the next moves.

'The killing is the responsibility of the local force; your involvement would not be welcome. Honestly, I think your task here is complete: Oluwaseyi is the end of the road for your investigations. If we discover any more fraudulent activities on his part, we will deal with them.'

Nick and Lesley had no choice but to agree, so the following day, they flew back to Lagos. Seated in Nick's office they went over the case again.

'The big question is – who killed Oluwaseyi? We may never know now we are off the case.'

The next day, Lesley and Nick both booked flights: Nick, to his next assignment in northern Nigeria, and Lesley, to Manchester.

* * * *

From his vantage point on the roof of the Chandler Hotel, Emil Jensen watched as Victor Oluwaseyi shook hands with his companion and left the café. Through his telescopic sight, Emil followed Oluwaseyi as he crossed the square. When he was sure no one was close to the walking figure, Emil squeezed the trigger and saw his victim fall. He quickly disassembled his weapon and returned it to its case. He gathered up the shell casing and made his way via the roof door, with its shattered lock, down into the hotel, and out to the car park. When he was safely on the outskirts of the town, Emil stopped his car and took a mobile phone from his pocket. He dialled a familiar number, and when his contact answered, he said, 'The loose end is tied up, Mr Levinson; enjoy your trip home.'

* * * *

DCI Caley and his family were packed, ready for the return home. The boys had loved their time with gran, seeing, once again, the island's glens and, of course, their favourite place: The Point of Ayre. As the family walked at the Point, Jack recalled that this area had started the police proceedings. Mrs Caley senior proved to be a willing babysitter, allowing Jack and Laura time for togetherness. They had seen so little of each other during the weeks of the investigation. Jack and the boys enjoyed watching the motorbikes roar around the Grand Prix course, and as a family, they had fun times together. Now, the time had come to say goodbye to Gran and the Isle of Man. With a promise to return at the next half-term, and cases loaded in the car, they headed for the evening ferry to Liverpool.

Sergeant Connor sent him regular text updates regarding the African programme; the last one he read informed him of the proposed trip to Johannesburg. The call from Connor arrived just as they were waiting to board the ferry. She informed him of the finding of Oluwaseyi and the shooting. And that the police general had decided that, with the death of Oluwaseyi, the investigation was over for her and Nick.

'I have emailed my report to your computer,' said Lesley, 'And I am now preparing to come home.'

'Thanks, Lesley,' Jack replied, 'I'm just about to drive onto the Liverpool boat. You can give me more details when we are back in Manchester; see you tomorrow, if you have recovered from your trip.'

On the ferry, Laura and the boys slept, while Jack pondered the latest news and wondered, 'Where do I go from here?'

September sunshine greeted Jack as, next morning, he left for the police station.

Sergeant Wilkes greeted him with, 'Good morning, sir. Welcome back.'

Jack was reading Sergeant Connor's report when she entered the office bearing two coffees, 'Nice to see you again, sir,' she said.

They sat at the desk, drank their coffees, and shared a little of their experiences.

'We will keep the rest for the super,' said Jack, 'We'd better go.'

The Superintendent spent the next two hours listening to the accounts and the results of the African, Isle of Man and Scottish investigations.

Following the conclusion of the reports, he said, 'From what I have heard it looks like case closed. I'll reserve my decision until I've read all your reports and discussed it higher up. Meanwhile, it's off to Salford for you, DCI Caley, and back to the grindstone for you Sergeant Connor; good morning.'

Back in his office, Jack phoned DI Lewis on the Isle of Man for an update on events there.

DI Lewis said, 'I'm up to date with your situation, courtesy of Connor's report, which she sent a few moments ago; the lady is on the ball.' Lewis then proceeded to report on the happenings on the island: 'Mr Levinson is on his way back to America, satisfied that the Ayre Project affair is done and dusted. Katy keeps me in touch with Jane. Oh, by the way, Simon comes home next week. The medical team is pleased with his progress.'

'Well,' said Jack, 'Unless the Super finds out anything to the contrary, I am reporting back to Salford tomorrow. For me, to be nearer home and family is a big plus. Perhaps we will meet up again when I holiday on the island; until then, au revoir, and take care.'

Jack shook hands with and said goodbye to Sergeants Wilkes and Connor and exited the Manchester station. He drove to Salford and checked in. Jack then rang Laura and apologised that he would not be home for dinner. He needed time and space to type a report from his oodles of notes and post them off to headquarters that evening.

'Wish me luck! Love you, darling. Don't wait up,' he told her.

* * * *

The bodies of James Walters and David Kingston were buried in a graveyard on the outskirts of Manchester. There was no clergyman present, and no one attended the burial. An unknown benefactor, however, erected headstones on the graves with just their names inscribed and at the bottomand – *Equinox RIP*.

Chapter 33 - Epilogue

An air ambulance flew Jane and Simon to the Isle of Man, and an ambulance waited to transport them to Nobles Hospital. As the driver opened the rear door, Katy waved from the entrance. When Simon's trolley arrived at the reception, Katy greeted them with hugs and kisses. Once Simon was through the necessary procedures and settled in his ward, Jane and Katy said goodbye and promised to see him later that evening.

Over the next two years, Simon's condition improved. He found himself able to help Jane and Katy in their successful B&B business, not so much physically, but administratively. Simon wished he could do more, especially as he watched his mother and Katy serving, washing and cleaning. In spite of all the hard work, their faces shone with pleasure and excitement; something he found difficult to comprehend.

Many customers stayed there, and not only in the summer, but at various times of the year. Kingsway became well known as an excellent B&B, with visitors from the UK, Europe and as far away as Africa.

Joseph brought Mila and his parents, and Jennifer came from Zambia with her new husband. Sergeant Lesley Connor spent a long weekend with them; Jane and Katy insisted she stay as their guest.

The Caley family, during their summer holidays, called in to say hello.

Graham and his wife and other friends from Craiglockhart Church spent time at Kingsway.

When, eventually, Simon received the all-clear to continue driving, he gained an abundant sense of freedom. Suddenly, he felt whole again; he realised that dwelling on his inabilities had hindered his capabilities. He grew stronger, physically.

On his knees, he apologised in prayer to his God, appreciating, once again, his great salvation. He earnestly sought the Lord's direction regarding the future; he longed, once again, to preach and to serve.

The answer came, one sunny afternoon, while Simon sat in the café at Niarbyl, one of the most beautiful scenic places on the Isle of Man. The wonder of God's creation engulfed not only his mind but his whole being. He found himself lost in adoration prayer.

'Excuse me.'

A voice jolted Simon out of his spiritual reverie.

'Simon Walters?'

Simon looked up at a familiar face: 'Kenneth!' he exclaimed.

The years melted away as he and Kenneth talked. Kenneth had married a fellow missionary in Uganda. They had three children: two boys and a girl. He told Simon of his appointment as Chief Superintendent in the new Methodist circuit, which included the Wirral and the Isle of Man.

'The Isle of Man, of course, has a local Superintendent, Vivien Mitchell, just recently appointed,' said Kenneth, 'And when I visited her yesterday, she expressed sadness about the diminishing numbers attending services in the chapels dotted throughout the island.'

'I know from my time living here,' said Simon, 'How parochial the Isle of Man can be. Quite honestly, growing up here, I loved that separate community spirit. I still love it today.'

'The point is, Simon,' continued Kenneth, 'I wish I had longer to stay this visit, but I travel back to Liverpool on the ferry this evening. Look, it is the very parochial mentality of our Methodist community that makes our meeting today monumental.'

'Wow! Monumental?' Simon laughed.

'Well, fortuitous, then.' Kenneth smiled: 'I want you to consider taking up the role of a lay preacher in the Methodist circuit, here on the island.'

At Kenneth's suggestion, a sense of spiritual joy flowed through Simon's whole being: body, mind and spirit. He uttered a silent prayer of thanksgiving to God.

'I think *monumental* was a great word to use, my dear friend,' said Simon, 'I feel . . . I must use the word *amazing* to describe the sense of a new door opening to me. The answer is a resounding *yes*! So, what happens now?'

'I will call with Vivien this afternoon before I leave and put your name to her as a prospective candidate,' said Kenneth, 'She will contact you and arrange a visit.' He looked at his watch, 'Oh dear, how time flies. Let's pray together.'

There in the Niarbyl sunlight, the two friends prayed, unconcerned about the strange looks from other diners.

* * * *

That evening, Simon read the history of the Methodist Church on the Isle of Man. He learned that Methodism first came to the Isle of Man by accident when, in 1758,

John Murlin was diverted there by a storm in the Irish Sea. Apparently, though, he had little impact on the island. The establishment of Methodism came via John Crook in 1775. Crook based himself in Peel, the fishing port situated in the west of the island. His main ministry was to the men and women associated with the herring fisheries fleet. As Simon continued reading, he discovered that John Wesley first visited the island in 1777. At the end of that visit, he wrote in his journal, 'Having now visited the island round, east, south, north and west, I was thoroughly convinced that we have no such Circuit as this, either in England, Scotland or Ireland.'

Wesley came back again in 1781 and, following that visit, his ministry became firmly established as the Methodist Church on the Isle of Man.

Closing his laptop, Simon deliberated on his future as a Bible teacher in the Ramsey Church, and his role, if it happened, as a lay preacher on the island's Methodist circuit.

The following morning, the Reverend Vivien Mitchell rang to arrange an appointment at her home. Simon had, as yet, not discussed his impending ministry with Jane or Katy, but at the coffee break, he broached the subject. The ladies were overjoyed, and they asked about Kenneth and how Simon knew him. He explained about college and his friendship with Kenneth there and told them about his friend's missionary work, marriage and family.

At 3 p.m. that afternoon, Simon presented himself at Vivien's home. He had met Vivien briefly at her installation, which was a relatively ecumenical occasion. Now, as she opened her door, he smiled and introduced himself. The Superintendent remembered having met him and knew of his accident and recuperation. They sat and talked informally, in her kitchen, with coffee. She explained the procedure regarding becoming a lay preacher and felt confident that Simon would have a future in ministry with the Methodist Church.

The following morning Simon wrote and forwarded his resignation to the church in Craiglockhart.

* * * *

Jane, Katy and Simon continued to attend the church in Ramsey where Simon led the mid-week Bible studies and occasionally preached. He was accepted for the Methodist lay preaching ministry, so visited and preached in several of the small Methodist chapels dotted throughout the island. Adrian, the Ramsey church pastor and his wife Madeleine, regularly visited Kingsway, enjoying home fellowship and Jane's cooking. Although the B&B had an excellent chef, Jane still enjoyed the occasional foray into the kitchen.

* * * *

The following year, Pastor Adrian had the privilege of marrying Katy and Simon; Joel's joking prophecy had come to pass.

And the Ayre Conspiracy? It was just a distant memory, which occasionally invaded their dreams.